T0209734

THE
HIDDEN HAND
OF GOD

JOHN PAUL &
ALLIE BLAND

BALBOA.
PRESS

A DIVISION OF HAY HOUSE

Balboa Press books may be ordered through booksellers or by contacting:

Balboa Press
A Division of Hay House
1663 Liberty Drive
Bloomington, IN 47403
www.balboapress.com
1 (877) 407-4847

Print information available on the last page.

ISBN: 978-1-9822-2136-2 (sc)
ISBN: 978-1-9822-2138-6 (e)

Balboa Press rev. date: 02/19/2019

Special thanks to,

Susie Rowland
Jon Holland
Jim Witmer

CONTENTS

CHAPTER 1

CHARLIE AND EVERETT INTRODUCED

The good news was the rain seemed to have stopped. The bad news was the rain had turned to sleet and was coming down so hard it ricocheted off Charlie's winter coat at an alarming rate.

Unfortunately, Charlie had selected a coat without a hood, which allowed the sleet to funnel down between his collar and neck. Again, he adjusted the collar to cease the relentless onslaught—again to no avail. The icy pellets trickled down the collar to his back. He already had doubts about what he was doing there and what exactly he was supposed to see. Humans, by nature, were skeptics. Some were blessed with an all-in faith, but most were skeptical. Charlie, even after all he'd seen, had reverted to his natural habitat of being a doubter. To Charlie, the trip had been unimpressive so far. Beside him sat his guide, Everett, who'd chosen an overly large winter coat, one with a hood that looked like a small carport.

Charlie glanced in his direction to see contentment on his face. Everett seemed to wear a permanent smile. Even if the smile and contentment took a short leave of absence, they were still there under the surface, ready to spring back to the top quickly.

As they sat on the cold park bench in an abandoned city park, Everett was happy. He whistled a tune so softly that Charlie had to remain motionless to hear it. It was a beautiful, mournful tune that was easy to listen to, even though Charlie had no idea what the song was.

Everett was perfectly satisfied with the seemingly dismal situation. To a person passing by, the scene must have looked odd: two men sitting on a park bench in the sleet, eating dessert. To Everett, though, it was a natural situation.

Everett scraped at the Styrofoam box, mining for the last morsel of banana pudding hidden in the corners. The plastic-on-Styrofoam squeal set Charlie's skin crawling. He turned in Everett's direction. Everett peered back out from his hood, his bright green eyes shining like those of an owl staring out from a country barn.

"How's your banana pudding?" Everett asked casually and nonchalantly, as if sitting at the beach on a warm spring day in April. Never mind that Charlie could now see the small pellets of sleet gathering around the laces and tongues of his shoes. Never mind that Charlie could see his pant legs had frozen in place.

Everett had spoken with such enthusiasm that Charlie felt obliged to reply with equal enthusiasm. "Boy, it's great."

Charlie had had some great desserts. The pudding was good, but to Everett, it was the best banana pudding ever.

Everett relaxed further as he spoke. "Sure is a nice evening, isn't it?" He again turned cordially to face Charlie.

As Charlie stared back into his face, he thought how cozy Everett looked inside his coat. No sign of frostbite. Everett smiled with each word, so instead of speaking what he thought, which was that he felt as if someone were pouring frozen BBs down his back and into his undershorts, Charlie said, "Sure is refreshing sitting here."

That statement seemed to spark Everett's enthusiasm. He sprang from his slumbering position and sat up straight. "You know, that's the word I was looking for: *refreshing.* Refreshing." He said it a couple more times just to see how it rolled off the tongue.

Charlie took another bite of his pudding just as Everett chose to congratulate him on his use of the English language. Everett slapped Charlie so hard that he bit his plastic fork in two.

"Refreshing. That sums it up in one word. Doesn't it, Charlie?"

Charlie smiled meekly back at him and then spit a small piece of plastic shrapnel into his Styrofoam container.

Charlie's name wasn't really Charlie. From their first meeting, he'd told Everett that repeatedly, but alas, Everett was determined to call him Charlie, and now Charlie had resigned himself, at least for the short haul, to being Charlie.

"Boy, Charlie, I can see why he sent you along. You're going to be a great help." Everett set his banana pudding on the bench and gave Charlie a hug so hard that Charlie could nearly hear his misaligned vertebrae clicking into place. Everett picked up his dessert container to continue his lovely evening of sitting in the sleet on a bench in a deserted park outside Trenton, New Jersey, when he made a discovery. "Would you look at this, Charlie? Can you believe this?"

On the bottom of the container was a card, which Everett held up to Charlie's face. "Buy four desserts, and get two free. Do you have one?"

Charlie looked under his container, but before he could answer, Everett clapped with excitement and said, "You do! You do!" The news had Everett rejoicing. "I wonder if we can combine the cards. Whaddya think, Charlie? Let's go back to get some more."

As absurd as it sounded to finish one dessert and then head back to the same restaurant to get another, Charlie immediately went for the idea. His teeth had started to chatter so violently he was afraid he might chip a tooth. To Charlie's disappointment, though, Everett did not get up; he sat back in his slumbering position and began to whistle the slow tune softly.

After running through the chorus of the same unrecognizable tune, he stopped, turned, and looked at Charlie's face. Charlie could tell by Everett's solemn expression and the serious look in his penetrating eyes that his happy-go-lucky manner had taken flight.

"Charlie, I know that what you see tonight will be hard to understand. It has always been hard for humans to see God working, but there are already things happening. The enemy is out in force. The opposition is obviously scared of the situation. The enemy will attack our saints; they have already attacked and discouraged. But we have a powerful warrior helping us." He then added with a smile and a hearty slap on Charlie's back, "You'll see. Hang in there. You'll see."

Charlie felt a wave of excitement course through his veins. That was why he was there.

He'd never seen Everett in his heavenly body, only as he appeared before him now. He knew Everett was an angel, with powerful abilities bestowed on him by God. He also knew Everett was not the kind of angel people referred to when they said, "Be an angel, and help me do this," or "Aren't you an angel?" Everett was an angel like the ones the Bible talked about: "For He will command His angels concerning you to guard you in all your ways; they will lift you up in their hands, so that you will not strike your foot against a stone" (Psalm 91:11–12 NIV).

Charlie studied Everett again to make sure he had not missed something, some hint of a heavenly being. Was there even a heavenly glow about him?

No. Nothing.

In fact, as he studied Everett, Everett's looks reminded Charlie of his seventh-grade science teacher. Everett was thin.

His graying blond hair was swooped to the side to give the effect he was not balding, but he was losing that struggle. His clothing choice was a ruffled-old-man look, which, to his credit, he wore well. His look would not have made one consider him strong, powerful, or a protector, which was what his name meant. In an arm-wrestling contest, most would have thought any seventh-grade girl could give him a run for his money.

Everett did, however, possess piercing green eyes that commanded attention. Once one looked into his eyes, he or she naturally wanted to know more about him. There was something that drew people in, beckoning for their attention—some instinct attracting them to him, a secret that drew them in. Perhaps remembrance.

Charlie knew the something he was drawn to. Love radiated from Everett—a deep love forever engrained into his being. It was part of his DNA, so to speak.

Charlie had experienced that love. That kind of love was God. Heaven pulsated with love; everything there was God's radiance. Charlie had been warned before he left heaven that he would be going back to a damaged world. The rotting evil would surround Charlie. The darkness of a fallen world would gather around him and rise from the ground like a smothering fog, showering him with choke-inducing dust. For the most part, that evil was the reason for humankind's heartache, but the evil stench could not fully penetrate Charlie's being. He had been bought and paid for. No other could lay claim to him.

The evil of the world had also been a battle for God's people, but Charlie had never seen evil through his new heavenly eyes. With his new awareness, he could feel evil and how it tried to latch on to anyone within reach. In their presence was a disturbance, and Charlie could hear the hatred for him from the hidden shadows. But he was only there as an observer. Charlie was there with Everett, the angel, the guide, who would show how the mighty hand of God worked in people's lives. It was one of the many stages Charlie would go through. He was being educated. He was on a journey—the slow passage humans took after death. Charlie had seen heaven, but now he would learn how almighty God worked on earth.

Charlie glanced at Everett, who had his eyes closed. On the face of the supposedly powerful angel was a serene, peaceful smile.

They glanced up to see a city bus skid to a halt at the stoplight. Apparently, the streets had become a little slick. As the bus belched out black smoke and continued its route, Charlie noticed someone had spray-painted "God is dead" on the rear of the bus. He considered that for a moment. He knew now that it took death to fully appreciate that God was indeed not dead.

He closed his eyes and happily recounted his journey from earthly life to his real home, heaven.

At the moment of his death, Charlie had felt as if he had come home. Immediately, he'd felt an overwhelming sense of love. It was not the kind of feeling one got when sitting down for a Thanksgiving meal at Grandma's. It was different. It was permanent.

Charlie knew the feeling would always be in him. The new type of love soaked into him. It permeated every fiber of his being. He could feel its intense warmth soaking into the inner fibers of his muscles and streaming through his body. He felt power coursing into the core of his being.

In heaven, Charlie remembered his past life on earth at least to some extent, because as soon as he arrived, he realized he felt no knee pain. Why would he even remember he'd had knee pain? The love had healed him of all his pain; all his sorrows were gone. All life's worries, he knew, were trivial in the presence of God. God had taken his burdens and felt the worry, the tension, and the pains of the world. Charlie felt the magnified power that forever would drench his every pore.

People on earth often asked, "If God loves us, why would he allow someone young, like Charlie, to die?"

When God created the world, he set up laws that governed the earth. When God created the earth, it was formless and empty. God set up laws to help form the earth, including the law of gravity and laws of chemistry, science, and physics. They were perfect laws, the laws of the land. God honored his own laws.

All of those laws had contributed to Charlie's death.

Could God break them? Yes, God could do anything he wanted. But there was comfort in knowing that God honored his laws. Charlie had learned that one should find comfort in knowing God's Word was the law. God was perfect. When he spoke, he always spoke the truth. When God said something, he honored it. God told humans he'd prepared a place for them in heaven.

The biggest question of mankind was the following: What happened when someone died?

Charlie had died on a Wednesday just like any other Wednesday. He was a sub mail carrier finishing up his mail route. He had just sorted out Mrs. Corletta's mail, checking to see if all the assigned fliers, mailers, and magazines were there. While getting ready to place her mail in her mailbox, he heard a loud bang, and that was it. No horrible pain. No fear. He could not speak for anyone else because he'd only experienced one death, but for him, there was no white light or feeling of rising—just a bang. He had been sorting the mail, and then he was on a beach, and at that moment, Charlie knew he had died.

Everett slapped Charlie on the back, stinging him back into the moment. They sat like two Eskimos in the blistering cold.

Everett knew humans. He knew they were terribly short-sighted. They could only see the small picture and were never able to see past one lifetime. That was just the way they were made. They were unable to understand the whole beautiful painting because they could see only one small brushstroke.

Because he loved it so, Everett softly whistled the same tune as before. It was his favorite melody of all the millennia. A nineteen-year-old Confederate soldier had composed it. The only thing the young man had ever wanted to do was compose music—that and make his mother and father, who taught music, proud. But alas, humans always wanted to kill each other, so amid running through cornfields, wading across rivers and creeks, and hiding facedown in the freezing mud while waiting for the blare of a bugle and the command to charge for the sake of killing his fellow man, the young soldier composed music.

Inside his shirt pocket, smeared with sweat and splattered with blood, was his lifework. Even when a cannonball cruelly tore off his leg in the Battle of Chickamauga, he composed. Leaning against a weathered pine tree, he frantically tied a tourniquet. He stopped the gush of blood long enough to finish his lifework. Even as he completed it, he knew no one would hear it. Still, he composed. The beautifully aligned notes spread onto the pages at an alarming rate as his blood drained out of his body. As the young soldier leaned there bleeding to death, he grasped that no one would ever see or hear his music. But he did finish his lifework. His father grieved till his own death that his only son would never experience life; he would never have a chance to see Paris, the ocean, or even the Mississippi River. The young soldier thought he hadn't accomplished anything in his life, until the moment of his death, when he realized that angels sang his music.

Everett softly whistled again, concentrating his powers on his next assignment.

CHAPTER 2

MARTIN THE BIKESMITH

Martin's Bikesmith had been in the same location for almost thirty years. Martin, the founder, ran the business, which he'd named Martin's Bikesmith simply because he couldn't think of a clever name.

Martin worked all the time. He enjoyed working. Since he was a kid, he'd been what the world called a go-getter. In the seventh grade, he doubled the sales of his closest competitor when selling candy bars to raise money for a class trip to Philadelphia. As a freshman, he set up his own business, repairing bicycles and skateboards. His grades suffered, but by the end of the year, he was making more money than most of his teachers. His reputation quickly expanded, and soon he couldn't keep up. He then set up an online parts store and hired a laid-off Campbell Soup Company employee, and the money poured in.

Martin had always had a loving relationship with both his parents. His father was a financial adviser at Merrill Lynch. His mother was a chemical engineer at Lockheed Martin. Together they earned a fabulous income and gave Martin a satisfying and loving childhood.

As the wind snapped at the awning above his storefront, Martin took a short puff on his cigarette, again annoyed with himself. He daydreamed back to the time when his parents had taken him down to Hilton Head, South Carolina, when he'd gotten the idea for his business.

While growing up, Martin had enjoyed traveling on nice vacations. His mother was an avid golfer. She had arranged a foursome to play one afternoon, so his father had made plans to rent bikes and explore the many riding paths with Martin. After their afternoon of riding, as they'd returned their bikes, Martin had strayed off to the side to witness rows of bikes waiting to be serviced. At that moment, something had clicked in his head, and he'd known he could learn how to service the bikes and build a successful business.

Martin loved both his parents, but he particularly admired his father. All through his youth, he'd looked up to his father. Whenever possible, they enjoyed a getaway to go hiking or biking. As of late, since his father had slowed down a bit, they enjoyed their time together collecting and researching antique toys. They both particularly enjoyed mechanical banks. Of course, like anything Martin touched, antique collecting turned into a money-making venture. However, Martin seldom sold any of the banks, because they gave his father so much pleasure.

Even though he had enjoyed somewhat of a privileged background, Martin worked all the time simply for the enjoyment of working.

Against the pleading of his parents, he'd paid his way through Thomas Edison Community College. His father, unbeknownst to Martin, put the money his parents would have spent on his college education into a savings account. After Martin graduated with a C+ average from the community college, his parents presented him with a check, and his father helped him find the commercial building where Martin set up his flourishing business. With financial guidance from his father, Martin kicked his business into high gear. What really set him apart from the average entrepreneur was his purchase of commercial properties throughout the eastern states. With his father advising and managing the investment properties, Martin was able to do what he really loved: repair bicycles. Nothing gave Martin more satisfaction than fine-tuning a high-end bicycle. With nine locations on the East Coast, he was always on the lookout for employees. He found it harder and harder to find quality help, so he worked late nearly every night.

Everett knew all this. He also knew that although Martin was happy, Martin had a vacant spot in his heart. Martin knew it too. After all the success, there was still something missing.

After writing up a receipt for a bike he'd just completed, Martin decided to stroll outside to the front of his storefront to check on the weather and smoke a cigarette. He hated that he smoked. He knew it looked foolish to own a business that promoted fitness and recreation and smoke cancer sticks, so he was somewhat of a closet smoker. For years, his mother hadn't even known he smoked. It wasn't until he was late in his thirties that she'd found out. Since then, she hadn't stopped harping at him to "stop that foolishness." He again thought about quitting.

As he walked out the front door, the cold wind bit into his face. He tried repeatedly to light his cigarette, but the northeastern wind was insistent on blowing the flame out. He thought about just forgetting about it, but never one to back down from a challenge, big or small, he quickly stepped back into the store to light his cigarette and then stepped back outside. With his small victory, he surveyed the weather situation and determined that it had all the makings of a full-fledged storm. He surmised he would be staying at his upstairs apartment, which would give him more time to finish up some bikes. He was constantly swamped but especially at that time of year, as his customers wanted to get their machines tuned up for an early spring ride. He glanced up the abandoned sidewalk to see two men strolling his way.

One, who appeared to be an older man, was walking with confidence, dressed in a quality parka. The other was a capless younger man tugging and fidgeting with the collar of his coat.

"Good evening!" Everett announced cheerfully.

"Good evening, fellas. What can I help you with?" Martin replied cordially.

"Well, I'm debating whether or not I want to update to the new Shimano electronic derailleur on my bike," Everett said.

Charlie looked at Everett as if he were out of his mind. Or maybe Charlie was losing his own mind. Why in heaven's name would an angel have any interest in a Shimano derailleur? And for that matter, how could an angel even know what that was?

Charlie again questioned what he was doing there, who this reject angel was, and how he'd gotten stuck with a dud.

Nevertheless, Charlie thought this little break might be a great time to shake out the ice from his collar and lower back. He tried to unzip his coat, but to no avail. He tried again with more force—still nothing. This time, he really went after it—but it still didn't budge. He reverted back to his high school days and voled off a string of pugnet profanities.

His outburst brought an instant glance and scowl from Everett, who, without missing a beat from his conversation, calmly reached for the snagged zipper and smoothly unzipped Charlie's coat. The incident brought both relief and frustration to Charlie. He was relieved to take the coat off and shake out the ice that had built up but frustrated that he couldn't even unzip a coat without backsliding to his olden days. It also didn't help that Everett had made it look so easy.

Charlie took out his frustrations on his coat. He shook the hated coat like a mongoose shaking the life out of a snake. Everett and Martin, who'd been chatting about the pros and cons of the latest electronic derailleur, both stopped to observe the assault taking place on the poor coat. When Charlie was satisfied with the thrashing of the coat, he put the coat back on and tried to zip it up, but alas, the zipper snagged on the way up. The snag immediately brought Charlie to a full boil, and he started mumbling insults to the coat again. Again, Everett, without missing a word from his conversation, scowled harshly at Charlie and smoothly zipped the coat up.

With the conversation between Everett and Martin wrapping up, as any successful salesperson would have done, Martin handed Everett a business card, made a final appeal for Everett to consider his business in the future, shook his hand, and said goodbye.

Everett placed the business card in his coat pocket and then whispered into Charlie's ear, "That went really well, Charlie. Don't you think?"

Charlie wanted to agree, but he didn't even know anything had happened. He was just thankful Everett didn't publicly chastise him for the vulgar language that had slipped out—twice.

Everett patted him on the back. "You'll catch on, Charlie. This is going to be fun. You'll see." With that, they stepped back out into the harsh wind—presumably, Charlie hoped, to go back to the café.

As soon as they left the bike shop, Everett hustled up alongside Charlie and gave him a side bear hug. Again, Charlie was amazed. For a scrawny little guy, Everett appeared to have the strength of a fifteen-foot python. Charlie gasped for breath; he thought he was going to have the life squeezed out of him.

Everett was excited. "That was a great accomplishment. Don't you think, Charlie?"

As he'd been for most of the mission, Charlie was confused. In his mind, the only thing they'd accomplished was some aimless talk about bicycles while the store owner lazily puffed on a cigarette. He'd been able to shake out the ice that had built up around his collar, but when he'd taken off the blasted coat, the harsh northeastern wind had thoroughly frozen him to the bone. On a positive note, he'd been able to fidget the most aggressive ice pellets out of his undershorts, so at least in the lower region, he felt a bit better.

Again, Everett excitedly side-hugged Charlie. Again, Charlie felt the lifeblood squeezed out of him, and as an added bonus, he was sure he could hear his shoulder joint give a pop.

"Yes, Charlie, they won't all be that easy. That was a great seed planted." This time, he gave Charlie a hearty slap on the back that sent Charlie stumbling forward. "Watch your step; the footing's getting kinda dicey."

Everett was so pleased that he started to sing quietly, almost dancing along the sidewalk, as the wind howled and again nipped at Charlie's face and ears.

CHAPTER 3

CHARLIE AND THE POSTAL WORKER

As they passed the next storefront, they saw a young lady cowering near the wall, huddled under the awning, trying to shelter herself. Charlie noticed immediately that she was wearing a postman's uniform, and she was sobbing. He looked to Everett. Surely Everett would spring into action and comfort the young postal worker, he thought, but instead, Everett abruptly headed back to the bike shop, explaining as he dashed back, "I've got one other question, Charlie. I'll catch up with you."

With that, Charlie's mighty angel was gone, leaving Charlie to fend for himself. Charlie awkwardly glanced over at the young lady, who realized she was being watched and quickly tried to compose herself. Charlie needed to make a decision: say something to her or walk away and pretend he hadn't seen anything. He weighed the options and then quickly spoke up. "Is there something I can do to help?"

The young lady, obviously embarrassed, meekly answered, "No, no, I'm okay." However, she immediately started sobbing again.

Charlie stepped forward and said, "I used to be a postal worker. Maybe I can help you."

The commonality brought a slight smile to her face. That smallest hint of trust opened the door, and she was desperate for help. "This is my first day on the job. I should have been done hours ago. I'm just so confused. I can't seem to find the last few addresses, it's getting dark, and I'm going to miss my train."

"Let me take a look. I can help," Charlie said, happy to find something he understood. He studied the last bits of bundled mail. He hadn't a clue where any of the addresses were but was determined to find them.

After the young lady composed herself a bit, she spoke up. "Thank you for trying, but I've convinced myself to go back to the office and resign after only one day on the job." Again, the flood gates opened, and she started crying.

Her tears brought a quick reprimand from Charlie. "Would you settle down? Give me just a moment."

She dabbed at her tears and tried again to compose herself.

Charlie wanted to curse at Everett again but suppressed the feeling. Instead, he thought to himself, *Where in heaven's name is that blasted angel? What kind of angel is he? I must have gotten the cut-rate model. When's he going to do something impressive? At this point, I would settle for remotely helpful.*

Charlie looked up and down the street but saw no sign of Everett. However, he noticed a door tucked beside the business they stood in front of, and above the door were two of the addresses he was seeking. As he studied the building, he noticed another door situated just down the alleyway, and above it were three more addresses. Knowing he had hit the address jackpot, he said, "I see five of these addresses already."

Startled by the discovery, the young postal worker looked up to see Charlie waving and pointing with enthusiasm. Relieved to know her route was almost completed, she squealed with delight. "I knew they were close. I just couldn't see them. I was so tired and frustrated I couldn't think straight. Thanks so much for helping." She grabbed the mail and shoved it into the boxes. "My name's Eva."

Charlie, still holding two more deliveries and surveying the street, absentmindedly answered, "Hi, Eva. I'm Charlie. Nice to meet you."

Temporarily forgetting he was frozen down to the marrow of his bones, he strolled down the street, looking for the addresses of the two remaining parcels. Eva began talking like a caged parakeet. "I had given up. The whole night has been like this. They're so short-staffed I barely had any training at all. This is my official first day on the job. Can you believe that? First day, and I'm out here by myself, wandering around like a lost pup. I was supposed to be done hours ago."

Charlie half-heartedly listened, but he was perturbed with himself for not seeing the last two addresses. He was even more perturbed that Everett was nowhere to be seen. He felt a fitting curse word trying to work its way to the surface but was able this time to show some self-control and suppress it. Eva had shifted into high gear on her narrative—something about her father getting the job for her. She wanted to do a good job. Charlie had wandered two blocks with Eva in tow, looking for the last two addresses. Finally, he spotted them and crammed the soggy mail into the slots.

With the task completed, Eva violently shook Charlie's arm like an eighteenth-century hand pump, apparently trying to get a few words out of him but receiving only a timid "It really wasn't that big of a deal; I knew all of them were close." Then, just like that, Eva said goodbye, thanking him profusely, and disappeared down the street.

Charlie, alone again, realized how cold and miserable he felt. He scanned the abandoned street for Everett but didn't see him, so he headed back to the bike shop.

Even before reaching the store, through the store window, he saw Everett and the store owner standing near a display of new bicycles, with Martin pointing and Everett nodding. Both were sipping cups of freshly brewed coffee or hot chocolate. Charlie felt his frozen lobster-claw right hand make a fist and imagined himself clocking Everett in the throat, but the image vanished immediately as Everett looked up and waved out at Charlie, again giving him a loving smile. Charlie, staring from the frozen cold into the toasty showroom, instantly felt his right hand work into a fist again, but he just as quickly loosened his grip as Everett tossed his empty cup into the trash, waved goodbye, and joined Charlie out in the elements.

"Okay, Charlie, let's keep moving. We have a lot to do tonight."

Charlie felt blood rushing to his face and ears and felt his blood pressure rising but said nothing, matching step with his holy guide.

CHAPTER 4

KAREN INTRODUCED WITH BACKSTORY

Karen was seldom unhappy, let alone depressed. Lately, though, she had been feeling downright dismal. First, she chalked up the depressing state to her age. Women of her age often experienced dramatic mood swings, at least according to magazine articles she had been reading. But she knew that wasn't it.

She had been through the dark tunnel of menopause and arrived safely on the other side. Besides, how could the men who'd written the silly articles really know about menopause? She didn't care how many studies they had conducted or how many women they had interviewed. Did they really know? She'd had the same thoughts some twenty-four years before when she read baby books written by men. Sure, they'd done studies, written papers, and interviewed women, but had any of them actually carried babies in their wombs or given birth to children?

She liked to run those questions through her head, bringing lofty doctors back to reality. Maybe she was having a midlife crisis.

"Don't be dramatic, Karen," she'd say quietly to herself.

She amused herself with that line. It was her mother-in-law's saying. Karen had adopted it years ago. Her mother-in-law said it to her often, but now the words helped her keep things in perspective.

Karen wiped the countertop of the café, even though it had not been used in half an hour. There was one usual customer at that late hour: Brian Michaels, a local city policeman. Brian stopped into the café as much as possible for his late dinner break. He'd always sit at the far end of the horseshoe-shaped counter, facing the door.

Looking at the deserted café, Karen thought about when she'd first started waitressing years ago, when the café had stayed busy up until closing. In fact, the evening shift used to be downright hectic, as the nearby factories provided a steady stream of customers hustling in and out on their dinner breaks. However, like many cities, Trenton had recently fallen on hard times. In fact, Karen, along with much of the help, wondered how long the little café would hold on. More than anything, she would miss the customers. She would miss sharing in their lives, rejoicing with them in triumphs, and crying with them in sorrows. She again thought of her parents and resigned herself to the cause of her slightly depressed state.

For years, she had lived knowing she had disappointed her mother and father. Both had passed on about three years ago. Maybe that was reason enough to be depressed. The anniversary of her father's death was next month. Was that just cause to be sad?

Karen, don't be so dramatic, she thought with a smile.

As she swept under the tables, reminiscing about being a huge disappointment, she realized her parents' disappointment never had affected her life. She was happy. It was evident to Karen that her parents had gone through life being miserable. Meanwhile, Karen had married her high school sweetheart, Jeffrey, known to most as Jay, whom she still adored.

Jay was the nice guy in school—not an athlete, the brain, the most likely to succeed, or even the best looking. All those accolades were cast upon her in high school. Karen shared several classes with Jay. She liked that he treated her with respect. He was easy to talk to, was a great listener, and worked at his father's garage after school and on the weekends. They casually talked in class but really got to know each other after school. Karen left the door ajar on her car one day, and Jay noticed her standing by the incapacitated car, obviously perturbed. He calmly assessed the situation and then sprang into action. After taking some jumper cables from behind the seat of his truck, he quickly had the car started. He then suggested Karen come by the shop, and he would clean the battery terminals. His selfless nature attracted Karen to him.

Some suggested to Karen that he was a nice guy but way below her social class, but she didn't care. When he invited her to the local demolition derby for their first date, she loved it. To Karen, the demolition derby was like a modern-day gladiator competition. She screamed till she was hoarse, and then he took her out for ice cream to soothe her inflamed throat.

The following weekend, he introduced her to his parents, who adored her. Karen loved them the moment they met. When they invited Karen to church, her life forever changed with the message of salvation. When she decided to accept Christ as her Savior during a Wednesday night women's meeting, her future mother-in-law was right beside her, crying, then laughing, and then crying some more.

Karen was so excited to tell of the good news that she burst into her parents' bedroom to share her life-changing event, only to be severely chastised by her father for believing in such a far-fetched fairy tale. Her mother completely ignored the news and sat up in bed to rebuke Karen for spending so much time at the home of "those hillbillies." She demanded Karen come to her senses and go out with Dr. Reynolds's son, who was head over heels about her.

Karen endured a forty-five-minute assault before finally calming her parents down by answering their onslaught of questions about dating and career choices with "I'll rethink my position."

But Karen followed her heart and dated Jay throughout high school and then throughout college at the University of Georgia, where both her parents were professors. She spent more time with her mother-in-law than her own mother, which was a mystery to her parents. Karen's mother-in-law introduced her to Jesus, the Holy Spirit, and the wonders of the Bible. The day Karen graduated from college, Jay proposed. When they broke the news to her parents at her graduation party, her father had to excuse himself because he was openly sobbing—not tears of joy. Her mother immediately took a Valium and was at least able to stay out by the pool to greet guests. When Karen went to check on her father, who was in the den, he was whimpering uncontrollably.

Karen had wanted to reprimand her father with a loud "Don't be so dramatic, Daddy," but looking back, she was thankful she hadn't. That also was not the best time, she later realized, to tell her father she would be having a quiet, small wedding with few guests and then moving to New Jersey, where Jay had taken a job working for his uncle, who owned a small trucking company.

To that day, she thought her father had wet his pants at the news, because after he regained his composure and rejoined the party, Karen saw that he'd changed from khaki to dark gray pants. For years, she hid the fact that Uncle Steve's trucking company had only two trucks. As distressing as those events were to her parents, things only got worse according to them. Barely a year after she and Jay were married, she was expecting.

Jake was born, and she had a new best friend.

With Jay being gone for long stretches at a time, the responsibilities of teaching Jake how to ride a bike, swim, and hit a curve fell to Karen. She was a champion pinewood derby builder, doghouse builder, and counselor on love and relationships to most of the teenage boys at Jake's high school. But she was not like the master fire builders she'd seen on YouTube. Looking back, she realized her first mistake was setting the tents up too close to the bonfire.

Jake had asked if several of his friends could camp out in the backyard, and Karen had excitedly accepted the challenge. She gathered twigs, obtained firewood, and researched fire building. Even though the wind was too strong to start a fire, she didn't want to disappoint Jake's young friends. Problems quickly got out of hand when sparks jumped from the campfire to one of the tents, which in turn set the next tent blazing. Soon the whole backyard was raging. Karen foolishly tried to rescue a guitar one of the boys had brought because he screamed and cried in a panic, "My grandpa's guitar! My grandpa's guitar!"

For her act of bravery in fighting the fires, Karen was awarded third-degree burns on one hand, had her sleeves burned off her sweatshirt, and had no eyebrows for a month. To that day, she received a scowl from the boy's grandpa every time he came into the café.

Karen wasn't taught any of those skills as a young girl, but she had found the essential tool of teaching herself. Whenever she needed to learn a skill set, she was never too shy to ask an expert, read a manual, or look it up on YouTube. She thought her crowning achievement was Jake's first car. He had saved every penny he touched from his odd jobs of mowing and helping people move and his birthday and Christmas money. One Saturday afternoon, Karen noticed a rollback truck stopped on the street outside their house. On the back was a poor excuse for an automobile. The doors were faded red, but the rest of the car gave hints that at one time it might have been dark blue.

Blanketing all the flat surfaces was a greenish mold. Poking from underneath the hood were bits of leaves. She sent up a quick prayer of mercy: "Please, Lord, don't let the neighbors park that terrible eyesore in their driveway." For good measure, she added, "You said, 'Ask, and it will be given to you,' so please don't let the neighbors park that monstrosity in their driveway."

As Karen busied herself wiping up the booths and tidying up, she smiled at the humor of God as she drifted back to that fateful day. She remembered the horror of watching through the window as Jake ran to the street, excitedly jumping about and pointing, and then reached for his wallet and handed the driver some money. She wished without hope that Jake had paid the driver to keep moving down the street, far from her house, but to her horror, she saw the driver hop into the cab and then back the eyesore into her own driveway.

After the deliverer of the wounded relic sped into the evening, Karen mustered her strength to see how bad the disaster was. As she timidly crept out, Jake charged at her excitedly, whooping and howling with excitement. "Can you believe it? Can you believe it, Mom?"

Karen's only response was "No. No, I can't."

Jake was so overcome with joy that he couldn't stop jumping and dancing. Karen was so overcome with grief that she couldn't move. She immediately wondered if she had a tarp big enough to hide the miserable train wreck.

Jake was already scrambling for tools and opening the hood. "Mom, it's a Mustang with a 429 Cobra Jet engine in it." To make sure she understood, he repeated the last line, speaking slower and louder: "A 429 Cobra Jet."

Jake might as well have been speaking Hebrew to her. She had no idea what a Mustang was, didn't know what the number 429 meant, and certainly didn't understand what a Cobra Jet was, but one of Karen's greatest traits was that she wasn't afraid to learn, try, fall down, and maybe look a bit silly once in a while.

During every waking hour for a solid month before Christmas, she and Jake rebuilt the engine. She knew nothing about engines or what rebuilding one entailed, but with the advice of a local speed shop owner who patronized the café, mountains of manuals, and Google, the engine roared to life. Everything went well until, when she was tightening the exhaust, a bolt snapped, and the ratchet cracked her in the left eyebrow; she was out as cold as a wedge. Jake rushed to the neighbor, who drove her to the hospital, where the eyebrow was shaved and replaced with thirteen stitches.

As the painkillers started to wear off the next day, she found herself riding shotgun in Jake's pride and joy, cruising down Highway 95, passing the Potomac River, on the way to Georgia to visit her family for Christmas. Even in her drugged state, she found it troubling that Jake had been driving for some four hours while she napped, considering he only had his learner's permit.

When they arrived, her eye was completely swollen shut, and she was wearing dirty work pants, with a nice combination of grease, oil, and transmission fluid under her nails. Even after she scrubbed up for an hour, the guests around the elegant dinner table looked at her as if she were the Creature from the Black Lagoon, but she and Jake had accomplished a great undertaking together. Despite the stares and mutters of the people around her, Karen was happy. She was proud. She loved her husband. She loved her son. She loved her life and was in love with God.

Everyone else around the table, except Jake, suffered from depression, high blood pressure, or alcoholism or was jealous of his or her neighbors or sleeping around.

Her parents never forgave her. Her father spoke to her one more time as she and Jake loaded up to go home. One last time, he reminded her that one of her sisters was a successful attorney in Atlanta and one was a fine architect in Memphis. She had wasted her time and their money by getting a degree from Georgia and an online master's degree from Georgia Tech. She had married a lowly truck driver who couldn't even take time off around Christmas. Her parents grieved that the best job she could find was as a waitress at a two-bit hole-in-the-wall café.

Even though the comments cut her down to her core, she hugged both her parents and told them she loved them. She also told them God loved them and wanted to have a relationship with them. She then got into the car and headed home. That was the last time she spoke to her father, who had a massive heart attack less than a week later. Her mother died six months later of a heart attack as well.

A loud crash from the diner's kitchen rudely jarred Karen back to the present. *Well, that sure was an enjoyable ride down memory lane,* she thought to herself. *No wonder you feel depressed. Everything you have done as an adult was unacceptable to your parents, and they're gone, so there's no way to ever please them.*

The bell above the door chimed with the arrival of two new guests.

Everett knew Karen had found great favor with God by counseling wayward teens, opening her home to all Jake's friends, being a mother figure to any who needed one, hugging those who needed hugs at the diner, visiting shut-ins, and bringing leftover pie to the VA hospital. Karen loved God. She was in tune with the Holy Spirit's leading. She was obedient. She went about her life without realizing she was a mighty warrior, a saint who was troubling the Enemy's plans.

CHAPTER 5

CHARLIE AND EVERETT IN THE DINER, AND CHARLIE MEETS KAREN AND BRIAN

A pleasant *ting-ting* from the bell situated above the door of the diner cheerfully announced Everett and Charlie's arrival from the harsh winter conditions. Charlie headed to a booth toward the back of the café to massage his feet back to life. He sat facing the rest of the diner as Everett sat at the counter to talk to Karen, who was cleaning up.

Charlie took off his coat and tried to undo the laces of his ice-covered tennis shoes. The laces were frozen together, so not to be denied, he kicked off the icy shoes. For a guy who was dead, his feet sure hurt. He rubbed some life back into his cheeks and shook the ice from the back of his neck. Fortunately, Charlie had chosen a booth where the heating duct poured a steady stream of hot air right on top of him. Unfortunately, the hot air smelled as if it were coming directly off the smoky grill, bringing a scent of the latest concoctions, which, as best as he could detect, were an egg sandwich and an order of hash browns.

Charlie's feet hadn't yet responded to the massage therapy, so he stuck them into the sleeves of his coat. He had upgraded the condition of his fingers from being as frozen as a statue to hurting and tingling, which was a good sign. He surveyed the café.

The little diner was dated but clean. The red tabletop of the booth was worn and brown around the edges. Charlie lifted the chrome napkin holder to reveal a love commitment carved into the tabletop. Faded but still visible was "SB loves CF." He wondered if SB was still in love with CF and if their romance had lasted as long as their defacing of property. Around the walls were various signed photos of celebrities who had eaten at the restaurant. Some of the photos, which had spent their existence in the direct sunlight, had not fared well and were discolored. It was obvious the stars in the photos had visited the café only once, since their photos had never been updated.

Even though the café was old and dated, there was a pleasant look to it. The city had grown up around that mainstay. Charlie could see the short-order chef vigorously scrubbing the grill in the back. Everett was casually speaking with Karen as she prepared their to-go desserts. The only other customer was a lonely policeman sitting at the counter. He had his head down, studying the sandwich and soup that were presumably his dinner.

Just as Charlie finished a thorough surveillance of the premises, Everett strolled over to the booth and sat down across from him.

"What do you make of the place, Charlie?"

Charlie pondered the question and started to count off the things he'd noticed.

Everett interrupted, holding up his hand. "No, I know all that. Do you see anything else?"

"No. Is there more?" Charlie said.

Everett's green eyes were bright and alert like those of a cat on the hunt. "Do you want to see what I can see?"

Before Charlie could respond, Everett continued. "The citizens of your former world are shielded. They are blind to the happenings around them. There are spiritual battles happening everywhere, Charlie. Some of your world chooses to be protected; some want to be a part of it. But they never actually see the battle raging. Part of your continued training, Charlie, is to see how the battles are fought and whom they are fought against. It is part of your teaching, your forever training of God."

Charlie said meekly, "Then I want to see, don't I?"

"Now, Charlie, there's no way to prepare you for this. You see, humans were never designed to see this. It is always around them, but they are spared. It's a little, well, different."

Without smiling, Everett reached across the table and firmly grasped Charlie's hands, and Charlie again felt the overflowing love he had experienced during his time in heaven. A kind warmness settled into his innermost being.

Everett spoke softly. "The feeling you have experienced is the eternal love of God flowing. Your kind has rejected God's love, so for a season, your former world is cursed. Look now on the curse that has polluted this world."

Charlie looked again around the café. The lighting was green, and a greenish-brown fog swirled around the room. What appeared to be giant flies swarmed around the policeman's head. Some landed on the back of his neck, biting and tearing at his flesh. Upon closer examination, Charlie realized the winged beings were some type of hideous creatures bent on tormenting and molesting the poor policeman. Some were walking on his back, digging and gouging with sharp talons. The policeman took no notice of the creatures, but as Charlie gazed into his eyes, he could see despair. There was a hollowness to the man's face. Sadness seeped from his eyes.

Charlie could now make out the sounds of the creatures crawling and flying about him. They were laughing at him. Some were hissing. Others, as they landed, spat on the policeman.

Everett said, "They are demons. Small demons of despair. They have worked on Brian for years. He has allowed it, and now they have a foothold on him."

"Why don't you stop them from this attack?" Charlie said.

Everett spoke barely above a whisper. "Brian has chosen to invite these demons in. He wants to live in his world of misery and despair. He has chosen for himself a life of discouragement. But by allowing these smaller demons in, he has opened the door for a more powerful demon to enter."

"But how did this happen?" Charlie asked.

"Brian was raised in the church, and at an early age, he asked Jesus to be his Savior. Brian grew up, went to college, married, and had a son. That son grew up but, at age sixteen, contracted a rare disease, which he died from four years ago. Brian blamed God. He blamed himself. He blamed Jesus. Instead of running to God for comfort and answers, he lashed out at God. Refused him and hated him. Brian would rather live in this murk and the darkness of this sewage than face God and ask questions to find his everlasting love and forgiveness."

"But what can we do to help him?"

"I'm here to shield Brian. He doesn't know it, but he has a mighty prayer warrior serving up prayers for him on an almost constant basis. This warrior is praying with much earnestness. God has heard the prayers. The warrior is trying her best to pray Brian back into the fold. But no matter what is prayed for him, he must make the choice. There are others who will be working in his life, but he must decide. Everyone has free will. Each must choose the side he or she serves."

Charlie glanced up to see Karen going about the business of closing the café. A small demon alighted on her back, and a frown suddenly appeared on her face. He turned to Brian, whose face was downcast. His shoulders had drooped, and he was obviously depressed. Charlie looked at Everett and said, "What do you mean these are smaller demons? Are there then larger demons?"

"Oh yes, much more powerful. There is a cunning demon on the way to destroy Brian. I am here to shield him. But he must accept this help, and our saint must continue her request to place us here."

"And if not?"

"Then Brian is left to fend for himself. He will probably continue to spiral downward till the evil engulfs him and takes his life. But there is help for Brian. He can pray for it. Others can pray for him or with him. Brian has someone praying intensely for him. See how the small demon has been swarming Karen? These demons are organized. They are cunning. They seek to torment. To cause discouragement and hatred. Their only mission is to lay claim to those of your world. They deceive. But they only have power that your kind allows them to have. Ones like Brian and Karen can have the kind of power that God has prepared for them only if they ask for it. All demons of any size or power must flee the presence of God. They cannot tolerate it. They cannot stand to be around the burning-hot love of almighty God." Everett released Charlie's hands, and the demons faded from his view.

Karen strolled to their table with their desserts packed neatly in a paper bag. She placed the package, along with the bill, on the table. "I signed your tickets. Next time you come in, you're entitled to two free desserts."

Her words brought a contagious smile to Everett's face. "Oh boy! You can't beat free," he said cheerfully.

She turned and went back to cleaning, and Everett slipped a pen out of his shirt pocket. He wrote something on the ticket, gathered some crumpled bills from his pants pocket, and spoke quietly again to Charlie. "The demons travel with Brian. Almost every hour, they torment him. These demons look for others they can attack. Karen will have none of that. She will dig into the Word. She will call her prayer warriors at her Bible study. She knows where her strength comes from. Brian has but a short time to decide whom he will serve. Our mighty prayer warrior will be coming home soon. Very soon."

Charlie gazed again in the direction of Karen, who sang as she filled the sugar containers. Everett neatly tucked the free-dessert tickets into his coat pocket, zipped up his coat, and patted the pocket for good measure. As he stood, he whispered into Charlie's ear, "Karen has a job to do. There is a more powerful beast coming through the door who is here to capture Brian tonight. I am here as a protector for Brian. Almighty God, through me, will protect him tonight. I will shield him. But Brian must decide whom he will follow and whose alliance he is pledged to."

Charlie watched as Everett took a seat next to Brian. He overheard Everett strike up a conversation about the weather, when the bell above the door chimed to life.

As if scripted, a finely dressed man entered the diner, as Everett had predicted. Charlie watched Everett eye the man who was supposedly a demon. The man appeared to be a successful businessman or maybe an attorney picking up dinner after working a late night. His coal-black hair was neatly combed back. He wore a black pinstriped suit that appeared to have been tailored to his muscular and trim physique. It was odd on such a cold, blustery night to see such a perfect specimen of a man.

The man coyly strolled up to the counter and took a seat.

Everett eyed the newcomer with suspicion. He knew this one. He could see him for what he was, but in the human world, others would see only a handsome man strolling into a café. Everett bristled at the sight of the deceiver.

Everett watched Karen, hoping she could see through the facade. He knew she had seen all types come through the door over the years. She had served celebrities who hid behind hats and glasses so as not to be noticed, New York athletes who yearned for a little greasy food that reminded them of home, and businesspeople who craved attention like spoiled children. Everett knew that type especially made Karen's skin crawl, perhaps because of her own background, wherein she'd been constantly around people who thought they were a bit higher up on the food chain than the common man on the street and felt more deserving of the finer things in life. That entitled attitude was especially revolting to Karen. Her family's years of training had led to the opposite of what they'd had in mind. That might have been why she was drawn to Jay. There was never any doubt what one was getting with Jay or his family. Their yes meant yes, and their no meant no. Karen especially admired that when her mother-in-law said she would do something, she would, even if it meant doing without. There was no playing the angles to benefit herself; no slick sales pitch ever rested on her tongue. What she lacked in money she made up for in work and prayers.

Politely, even though it was minutes before closing time, Karen walked to the handsome man and asked what he might like. He asked what dessert was still available and ordered a coffee to go.

"Good girl, Karen," Everett muttered softly. He watched the newcomer survey the small diner like a hungry wolf. His eyes systematically studied each seat.

I see you, demon, but tonight you won't see us, Everett thought. He knew the world would see only a policeman sitting in a café while eating his dinner and having a light conversation with an older man sitting next to him. They could have been discussing last night's basketball game or the weather. The world would see the old man lightly chuckle and then pat the policeman on the back and possibly wonder why the old man left his hand on the policeman's back a bit too long but assume the lonely old man just wanted some human contact.

In reality, Everett drew his powerful shield up to cover Brian, to shield him from the view of the evil spirit bent on destroying the policeman.

Karen was quickly preparing the dessert and coffee to go.

The demon again scanned the diner, but when he came upon where Everett and Brian were seated, he gazed over their places without taking the least amount of notice, as if they were hidden from his view. The handsome man slowly surveyed the café, scanning the seats as a hawk might scan fields for weak prey to devour.

Everett knew his cover was solid at least for the evening. He felt the evil radiate from the strong demon, and he studied the hunter of the weak. Everett knew his adversary: he was looking, poised, ready to attack. But no prey was on the horizon that evening for the predator. The stranger made small talk with Karen as he stood up to leave, examining the surroundings. Everett sensed a hint of panic in the eyes of the crafty wolf.

I know you must now answer to your greater power, Everett thought. He watched the man gather the package and stroll out of the warmth of the café into the blustery night wind.

Charlie looked to Everett, who was standing next to Brian at the counter. Everett heartily patted Brian on the back, and for the first time during the encounter, Brian smiled, reached out to Everett, and firmly shook his hand. Everett grasped the handshake, looked directly into Brian's eyes, and spoke softly.

Brian laughed and said, "Stay warm."

With that, Everett thanked Karen again and motioned to Charlie that it was time to leave. Everett knew something was changing, however. There had been an awakening of sorts. Some evil had been stirred. He knew evil had been threatened.

CHAPTER 6

DEMON SCENE

The man who had visited the diner lay writhing in pain in a dark cavern far beneath the city. He staggered to his feet once again after being picked up and hurled against the wall by a presence hidden in the shadows of the clammy cave. The man spat out the dirt he had lapped up from the dusty floor.

A demonic voice growled, "I asked you for information, and you bring me nothing."

The once sharply dressed man shrieked out a desperate cry, "I don't know! There was no one in the diner other than the two working. The ones you seek must be hidden under a powerful cloak of immunity."

That statement enraged the large demon, who slinked from the darkness. Racked by centuries of hatred and evil, the demon's limbs were twisted. A liquid that appeared to be sweat seeped from the pores of the demon's body, giving it a permanently greasy texture, but it wasn't perspiration: it was hatred. He raised a crippled limb to brutally slap the man again. His name was Drakius. He was so enraged that he grabbed the man by one ankle and effortlessly flung him viciously against the cave wall again. Drakius then started his rant. "I need to know who they are after, and I need to know where they're going. I sent you to

35

find out, not to stir up a common waitress and a cook. You fool, you have only alerted them to our presence."

Irritated, he grabbed the man by the neck and pinned him to the cave wall with his forearm. He then lightly scratched at the man's cheek with the razor-sharp talons that protruded from his clawlike hand. "I asked for simple answers. You have failed."

The man watched helplessly as the blackish-blue finger picked cruelly at his flesh. He watched as the needlelike fingernail picked at the corner of his eye. He felt his eye throbbing under the pressure. Playfully, the demon traced around his eye, lifting his eyelid, running the pointed fingernail under his eyelid, and letting it snap back. The man could taste the thick, rotten breath of his torturer as the beast's tongue flicked at the wounds on his cheek.

The taste of fear excited the large demon, who scraped viciously at the man's cheek and neck. The doomed man let out an agonizing scream, which further excited the large demon. Crazed with excitement at the display of fear, he savagely bit the man's forearm. Hungering for more, he seized the entire arm in his mouth. He was tempted to crush it off with his dagger-like teeth but resisted. The large demon backed away from the once proudly dressed figure who had marched smugly into the small diner. Drakius lurked back into the shadows of the cave to pout.

He bellowed, "Go back! Bring me a soul tonight."

CHAPTER 7

CHARLIE MEETS CASEY
AND THE ALLEY KIDS

As Charlie stepped out of the diner, he immediately noticed that the north wind had picked up considerably. The freezing rain had become a steady snow as the temperature dropped. Everett seemed to know where the two were heading, because he stepped out of the diner with a new zeal.

"Come on, Charlie. Let's get to the train station."

Charlie thought, *Where would we be going on a train? And why take one anyway? He's an angel. Everett should just magically reappear, shouldn't he?*

They quickly headed north up the sidewalk, directly into the fierce wind. Everett proudly tucked the dessert sack under his arm as if it were a prize pig he had won at the fair. Even for a city as large as Trenton, the streets were sparsely traveled, partly because it was a Monday night in the middle of winter, and the forecast predicted there was an ugly storm brewing. The sidewalks were even less crowded than the streets. At some stretches, the going was downright dicey. After two blocks, Charlie and Everett headed west for a block but then turned south, away from the wind. Everett again was under his vast hood, which served nicely as a porch, shielding him from the snow and blocking the wind. Even though it appeared they were traveling in circles, Charlie tried his best to keep calm and keep his mouth shut.

Everett seemed happy and unaware of the danger of the peculiar path he was leading them down. He was cheerfully singing the same sonnet he'd whistled earlier, while Charlie was back to struggling again with his collar, adjusting and readjusting it. He finally resolved himself to the fact that his ears would develop serve frostbite and then blacken and fall off to the ground somewhere in an alley in Trenton, New Jersey.

Giving up on the collar, he decided to concentrate all his efforts on saving his fingers and toes. He tried crinkling his toes up into his shoes, which helped to a point but made it hard to walk at any decent pace. His fingers dove into the farthest corners of his pockets, burrowing into what warmth they could find.

Everett stopped quickly and faced Charlie. "Well, are you ready to see the mighty hand of God in action?"

Before Charlie could say anything or even nod, three characters turned out of the alley, blocking their path. The oldest appeared to be in his late teens and was wearing a lightweight New York Giants hoodie with sleeves tattered at the cuffs. His unwashed, ragged jeans suggested he had been living on the street or, at the most, in a shelter. The other youths were not dressed any better. One was carrying a bottle wrapped tightly in a paper bag. The other was dangling from his side what appeared to Charlie to be a wooden table leg. Glimmering under the dim streetlights was a large knife held by the eldest. The two youths were obvious followers of the older boy.

The oldest boy stepped into Everett's path, drew the knife up to Everett's eye level, and said, "Let me get right to the point, pops. You see, we're hungry, we're cold, and we're broke."

Charlie noticed right away that the attacker possessed not the East Coast accent he had expected but more of a southern twang. Even though Everett was being threatened, Charlie could tell by the sound of Everett's voice that he was still his same happy-go-lucky self.

Everett told the boy, "Well, yeah, I can see you must be freezing in that lightweight jacket. And I tell you, boys, I just saw the weather forecast, and it's supposed to get a heck of a lot colder before it gets warmer. I heard there could be a real nasty storm developing in the next few hours. Ice turning to heavy snow accumulation. And as we can now see, the ice has certainly turned to snow. I can feel that the temperature has dropped even in the last hour."

"Shut up, ya stupid old man! We didn't stop you to get the weather forecast!" yelled the oldest boy. He then scraped the knife blade against Everett's throat, which brought a chorus of laughter from his sidekicks, who felt the courage to chime in with suggestions.

"Teach him, Case."

"Yeah, get his money, and let's get outta here, Case. I'm freezing."

Case, fueled by the encouragement of his peers, pressed the knife into Everett's neck, gingerly rocking the blade on Everett's jugular vein.

The action did not extinguish Everett's cordial and friendly manner. He politely said, "Case? Is that Mr. Case? Or is Case short for Casey?"

The words enraged the teenager further, and he spat out a rash of profanities.

Undaunted, Everett continued. "We have no money, Casey. Zero. None. Not a penny between us. But I can give you this nice parka, and my friend Charlie has an equally nice winter coat."

Everett casually took a step back from the menacing knife blade. Casey seemed a little amused by the nonchalant attitude of his victim, and he dropped the knife to his side as Everett unzipped his winter coat and took it off.

Charlie studied Everett as he willingly handed the coat to the kid who, seconds ago, had had a knife to his throat. The parka had been hiding Everett's fragile earthly appearance. He stood there in his light blue cardigan, and heavy flakes of snow quickly turned the sweater into a patchwork coat of many colors. His belly pouched out slightly. His shoulders sagged. To the human eye, he appeared to be a ninety-eight-pound weakling grown up and over the hill.

Once Everett had his coat off, he held it up at arm's length and enthusiastically said, "Now, Casey, you wear this coat, and I guarantee you will stay toasty warm. The hood is a great addition; it protects from those lousy north winds we've been experiencing the last couple nights."

The youths were dumbfounded. One stepped forward to examine and touch the material of the coat.

Everett continued his sales pitch as the snow started to really come down. "It has two sets of pockets, one with zippers, and I believe—" Everett examined the coat again. "Yes! It's reversible!"

The boy who had come up to examine the coat said, "It is a nice coat, Case."

Case turned on the boy. "Shut up, stupid. We're not at Dick's Sporting Goods, picking out a coat for a ski trip. We're robbing these old men so we can eat."

Charlie's ears pricked up. *Old men? Who are these kids calling old men?* He wondered when Everett was going to whip out the golden sword and cut the thugs in half.

Everett, however, started up the sales pitch again. "Well, I can help in that department too. You see, we just came from the diner a few blocks away, and we have two desserts you can have." He lightly touched the side of the sack and then confirmed with a nod and smile, "Still warm!" He turned to Charlie and asked him to take off his winter coat.

Charlie hesitated, which brought a heavy scowl to Everett's face. He reluctantly obeyed Everett's obvious body language, relinquishing the coat with which he had a love-hate relationship. He now stood in the howling wind in a faded yellow T-shirt. The wind lifted the shirt up like a sail, exposing his skin to the snow and wind, while Everett was still engaged in closing the sale, helping one of the boys into Charlie's coat.

Turning the boy around, Everett checked for a snug fit. "That looks nice on you—a real nice fit." He patted the boy heartily on the back. "Even in Giants colors. Blue and white. We happen to be Saints fans. Aren't we, Charlie?"

Everett turned to Charlie with a wink and a smile, but Charlie was seething. Everett had given away their coats and their desserts, even though Charlie knew Everett could easily have crushed the three hooligans.

Everett turned back to the three youths. Two were wearing the beloved coats, while Charlie stood in a developing blizzard like a hairless cat.

"I have one last bit of advice for you three," Everett said.

Charlie inched closer, ready to see Everett at his finest. He was going to show them who was boss.

"A life of crime is no life at all, Casey. You are breaking your mother's heart. You will be arrested shortly, but turn your life around. Make something of your life; don't squander it. The police are on the way."

Enraged, Case got in Everett's face and said, "Crazy old man, we're not getting caught. What makes you think the cops would be out on a night like this?"

Everett nonchalantly pointed up the street. "Because I see them heading this way."

Charlie turned to see a squad car with lights flashing heading their way. When he turned around, the boys were dashing down the alley from which they had come.

Now, Charlie had been to heaven and seen the glory of God. He'd felt the everlasting love that abided there. But for some reason, he became like a spoiled kid who pouted and cried when he didn't get his way.

Like most of mankind, he couldn't see long term. He still didn't understand that God could use any evil event for good. He immediately forgot that he and Everett were on a mission and that God had a plan for each of them. God loved the lost youths struggling on the street as much as he loved a minister in the pulpit.

Charlie's adrenaline started pumping. Witnessing Everett's lack of effort, being on the verge of frostbite, and seeing his winter coat head down the alley without him in it infuriated Charlie. Something inside his new human body switched off, and for no logical reason, he grabbed a loose two-by-four lying by a nearby dumpster and charged down the alley after the fleeing juveniles—no logic and no plan, just spur-of-the-moment stupidity.

Everett chased him, shouting, "Charlie! Charlie, come back!"

Less than halfway down the dark alley, Charlie tripped over a manhole cover and cartwheeled head over heels, breaking his fall with his knuckles and forehead.

Everett caught up to Charlie, and instead of asking how he was, he asked, "What in heaven's name are you doing? Why would you chase three guys down an alley over a used coat and some banana pudding?"

As Charlie saw blood dripping onto the fresh snow from his throbbing forehead, he wondered the same thing. The policeman Everett had prophesied would arrive did indeed arrive and ran toward the fallen man.

"Where has he been shot?" the cop asked.

"Nowhere," Everett answered calmly.

The policeman then asked, "Did they knife you?"

Everett calmly said, "No, sir."

The policeman then coolly spoke something into his handheld radio and knelt to quickly assess the damage. He then headed back to his squad car with Everett in tow, chattering to the officer.

Charlie lay in the snow, assessing the damage. He felt as though he must have tried to catch himself with the knuckles of both hands. The skin was worn completely off three of the four knuckles of each hand, leaving only the pinkie unharmed. His pants were torn open at the knees, revealing nasty scrapes. Thankfully, though, Charlie's face had stopped the fall.

Everett and the policeman returned to help Charlie to his feet, and the policeman chastised Charlie for his foolish actions. "Do you know how crazy you are to chase three thugs down an alley? All for the sake of a used winter coat?"

At that point, Charlie expected Everett to defend his actions. Instead, Everett said, "Well, they also got our dessert, Officer. I'm sure you've been to the café just up the block. We had a couple of banana puddings to go. Excellent. Very tasty."

The police officer nodded enthusiastically. "Oh yeah, great place. If you ever get a chance, try the peach cobbler. Karen working tonight?"

Everett said, "Sure was. Nice lady, and how personable."

The officer nodded again. "Yeah, Karen's a sweetheart. My boy played hockey with her son. Nice kid." He looked at Charlie. "Well, let's get you up and over to the squad car to have a better look. Can you stand?"

Charlie thought that was a silly question, but as they helped him to his feet, he began to feel light-headed. The excitement and the sight of his blood on the fresh snow made his legs feel wobbly. His head swam, and the alleyway spun. He felt nauseated, and the big dessert he'd wolfed down didn't help. He dropped to one knee. He could feel banana pudding working its way to the top. He thought to himself, *This doesn't seem like the almighty hand of God I expected.*

Charlie awoke a moment later with Everett right in his face. "Charlie! Wake up, boy!"

Looking around, Charlie found himself sitting in the backseat of the squad car with his feet hanging out in the snow and a large blanket wrapped around his shoulders. A cold blast of wind snapped him back to reality, along with Everett repeatedly saying, "Charlie. Charlie. Charlie?"

The police officer came up to Everett and asked, "How is he?"

"He's fine," Everett answered.

"I have an ambulance on the way."

"No, I don't think that is necessary. Do you, Charlie? How you feeling? You okay?"

Before Charlie had finished assessing himself, he heard his mouth blurt out, "No, no, I'm fine. No problems at all."

"Well, if you two want to hop into the back, I can give you guys a lift if your destination is relatively close."

As the policeman made a call on the radio, Everett whispered into Charlie's ear, "Charlie, you have to trust me. You must trust God. What's wrong with you? You have seen the glorious side of God. You are here to see God working."

Charlie's knuckles were now throbbing. Again, his doubt, discouragement, and sense of being abandoned by God tipped the scales against the love he had experienced. Without thinking, Charlie blurted out, "Everett, if you're such a powerful angel, why did you let those thugs rob us? This whole evening, you have done nothing to show me you have an ounce of useful power. I have seen nothing to even remotely resemble God working here."

Everett smiled slightly. He could feel the discouragement, sense of loss, and sense of abandonment. He knew. Humankind was short-sighted. As the snow blasted down and the warning lights of the squad car circled the walls of the abandoned buildings, he firmly placed an arm around Charlie and whispered, "Charlie, this evening is for you. You are witnessing the hidden hand of God. Don't quit on me. You are going to be amazed."

Charlie huffed. "I don't see it. I'm not amazed. I'm cold, wet, discouraged, and bloody. How am I supposed to see? How?"

"Charlie, trust me. Trust God."

With both passengers strapped in, the squad car slipped and slid away. Charlie leaned his throbbing head back on the seat and then concentrated all his efforts on convincing his dessert to stay where it was and not end up on the floor of the squad car. Everett and the officer chatted away.

"You know, back to talking about the café, all the force seems to eat there," the officer said. "Really get a good meal for the price."

"Yeah, we saw one of your team in there tonight, eating his dinner," Everett said. "I spoke to Brian just a bit. Poor guy acted like he had just lost his best friend."

The officer said, "Sadly, you're not too far from the truth. This is an awful time of year for poor Brian. I think it's been four years now since he lost his son. Also during the heart of hockey season. You know when you hear someone say, 'So-and-so could make it at the pro level' about some sport? I'm here to tell you if any kid was ever to make it at the pro level in hockey, it was going to be Brian's son."

The good thing about traveling with angels was that they sensed what one was thinking or feeling. Everett kindly placed his arm around Charlie and gently nudged his head to rest on his shoulder. With the lightest pressure, he stroked Charlie's throbbing temple, and Charlie could feel his pain retreating. As Charlie relaxed, he could feel the love flowing from Everett. Feelings of his beloved papaw flooded over him. He could smell the freshly cut hay on his overalls and the peppermints Papaw seemed to always have an endless supply of. He felt Mamaw caress his cheek with her flour-scented hand. He could hear her whisper into his ear, "Honey, you and your papaw get cleaned up for supper; I made you a surprise," which meant she had baked a fresh apple pie that was still warm in the oven. After supper, she would cut him a large slab. Together they'd sit on the creaking porch swing, watching the lightning bugs and listening to the songs of the whip-poor-wills.

Charlie closed his eyes, absorbing the warmth and love that flowed from his guide, whom he had just insulted and doubted.

The officer continued with his story about Brian's son. "That kid was light-years ahead of any kid I ever saw skate. I'm not saying that just because the poor kid's not with us. I mean he was the real deal. Simply took the will to live out of Brian when the poor kid died. Everyone who knew the kid died a little, but Brian never rebounded. I know you never get over something like that. I'd probably be the same, but it's gut-wrenching to even be around Brian—even now, I'm sorry to say. Simply took the life out of him," he repeated, wagging his head sorrowfully. "Poor Brian used to talk on and on about hockey during the season, but since his son died, he never even mentions it. I've heard he's not been to a game or watched one on television since. Poor Brian." He skidded the squad car to a stop in front of the train station.

They thanked the officer repeatedly and then headed into the warmth of the station.

CHAPTER 8

EVERETT AND DRAKIUS

Angels weren't born. Angels weren't humans who died. Humans did not become angels; angels were completely different entities. Angels were created. They were created to do the works of God. They were created by God for God.

Long before the earth was established, there were angels. Long before the creation of the farthest stars mankind could fathom, angels were doing the work of God. There were two angels God created at the same time. He named one Everett, and he named the other Drakius. They weren't really brothers, since angels were not born and did not have families, but from a human standpoint, they might have been considered brothers. Unlike humans, angels did not grow up; they were created the way they were for what they would do. However, like humans, they faced choices. They could make right decisions; they could also make wrong decisions. They were equipped with a much better understanding than humans. For example, they were more hardwired to the will of God. They had a better understanding of what was right and what was not right. They were designed to feel the intense love of God coursing through them. Therefore, God dealt with angels more harshly than with humans.

Long before the earth was created, there was a terrible and heartbreaking disturbance. One of the angels, Lucifer, was much beloved by God. He was trusted and given much power. He was favored. Because of the intense love God had for Lucifer, he gave Lucifer a gift: the ability to create. Lucifer found great satisfaction in doing a good job. However, because of his mighty powers and knowledge, he began to think too highly of himself. Lucifer accomplished a lot and got more and more satisfaction from what he did. Because of his enormous pride in his accomplishments, he began to change.

Lucifer began to distance himself from God. He began to compare himself to God. He began to see himself as mightier than God. He quickly grew in power and pride—so much that he devised a plan to overthrow almighty God himself. Lucifer created evil. He wanted to be not on the same level as God but above God. He wanted God to worship him. He wanted the God who'd created him to bow at his feet. He gathered his army of angels. He deceived, lied, and promised, all to satisfy his raging pride. He wanted more. He wanted others to worship him.

As two angels who always worked together were coming from the throne of God, Lucifer confronted them. "Aren't you busy? Scurrying here and there, but for what? Why do you tire yourselves so? Who benefits from your labor?"

One of the angels immediately sensed a disturbance. He instantly felt a new sensation: caution.

Everett backed away from Lucifer but spoke boldly to him. "Lucifer, why do you try to sow seeds where they aren't wanted? Why do you question what we do? We gladly do the bidding of our almighty God. It is not labor; it is pure joy. Why do you suggest we tire in our tasks? You know we neither tire nor grow weak in our responsibilities."

However, Lucifer, in his craftiness, saw in the eyes of Drakius that doubt had been planted. He knew doubt could grow. The smallest of seeds was what he needed. He said to

Drakius, "Come with me, Drakius. Let me show you what I have created. Let's leave Everett to his mindless toils. Walk with me while we rest. What harm is there in resting? Let's go view all I have done."

Drakius turned to walk with Lucifer, and as he did, the small seed of doubt blistered into jealousy.

Everett, at first confused by the new and strange sensation of caution, felt a terrifying new feeling: evil. He turned to Drakius. "Come back with me, Drakius. You know our instructions. You know we have a job to do. You know we do not need to rest. Come back with me to finish our tasks."

Drakius laughed and said, "You go. You work. You labor in vain. I have found a new way. Lucifer has shown me a new path."

As Everett turned to leave, he felt another confusing sensation: sadness.

CHAPTER 9

THE ARREST OF CASEY

As cocky kids sometimes did, Casey and his two counterparts made a critical mistake. They raced down the alleyway, laughing and taunting the officer who was trying to arrest them. In their youthful minds, the bumbling idiot who chased them down the alley helped them. After tripping over a manhole cover, he bounced his face off the alley's floor, which sent the minors howling with delight. Pleased with themselves, they stood near the end of the alley, casting insults and mocking the officer.

"What's wrong, copper? Can't a pig run on ice?" Casey yelled at the top of his voice.

Casey happened to be quite clever. His scores in English and vocabulary were exceptional. In his high school speech class, he'd shocked his teacher by delivering several complex and convincing speeches. His clever insults, however, were lost on his sidekicks.

"Why would a pig be on the ice, Case?"

Casey looked toward his subordinate and scowled but said nothing. The youth, after the visual scolding, tried to redeem himself by shouting his own brand of insults, which mainly involved cursing and repeating what Case had said. Unbeknownst to the youthful thugs, another police officer now stood at the entrance of the alley, blocking their exit.

The youths continued their onslaught of insults and jeering with their backs to the officer. When they tired of their insults, they turned to see the officer with his nightstick drawn. The two younger thugs panicked, but Casey sprang into action.

"What's the problem, Officer? We're just returning home tonight after stopping by the diner to bring home some dessert for my mother. She's been working late lately, so I thought I would bring her home a treat."

The officer said, "Oh, you've been just down the street to the diner?"

Casey, feeling encouraged, continued. "Oh yes, Officer, we've been down there for close to an hour. We had dinner, and now we're just walking home. That's the truth, Officer. I swear."

The officer calmly spoke into the radio strapped to his shoulder and then said, "Now, boys, we've had some reports of young men fitting your description vandalizing some buildings, and my colleague says you robbed two men of their valuables. Is that true?"

Casey said, "Oh no, Officer, completely untrue. I can assure you we have been at the café for well over an hour. That was not us."

At that point, a new squad car pulled up, and two additional officers got out. The younger of Casey's two toadies then made another foolish mistake. He looked the officer square in the face and said, "Yeah, and we didn't take no valuables. All's we gots were these coats!"

Casey pinched the bridge of his nose and mumbled, "Thanks, genius."

At that point, the second toady decided he should run for it. He was particularly slow of foot and was rewarded for his feeble attempt by being tossed up face first against the cold bricks of the alleyway building. Casey, realizing his cover was blown, lashed out against the arresting officer, hurling insults and showing signs of aggression toward the officer.

The officer sighed and rubbed his aching temple, thinking to himself, *Why do these kids make everything so hard?* Then he calmly said to Casey, "Settle down. We just want to get to the bottom of this. Don't insult me or my colleagues; you're just adding to your troubles. Show me some ID, we'll go down to the café to confirm your story, and you can be on your way."

There were several scenarios that could have played out. The teens could have come to their senses, resigned themselves to the authorities, taken the medicine the officers dished out, begged for forgiveness, and probably been on their way. Instead, one, the least fleet-footed of the group, had unwisely tried to make a run for it, and Casey chose to become unruly, verbally combative, and borderline physically combative with the officers.

Brian, the first arresting officer, knew the three kids were guilty. He would rather have severely chastised the youths and had them promise to head home and stay out of trouble on that miserable night, but when Casey got out of hand, Brian had to tase him.

As Casey lay facedown on the snow, quivering from the shock and the cold, the reality of the situation began to set it. All the years of fighting with his mother and the anguish of being uprooted from his family and friends in Jackson, Mississippi, and sent to a completely new environment crept to the surface. He recalled the words recently spoken to him. The prophetic words of his victim echoed in his ears: "A life of crime is no life at all, Casey. You are breaking your mother's heart. You will be arrested shortly, but turn your life around. Make something of your life; don't squander it." How could that crazy old man know him—or his mother, for that matter? Who was that guy? As tough as Casey wanted to be, after all those years of putting on a defiant face, it seemed too hard to be resilient anymore. Casey began to cry.

CHAPTER 10

KELSEY THE JANITOR AND BACKSTORY

Everett understood. He knew humanity. He had seen multitudes of people throughout the ages. All of them were searching, and none were sure what they were searching for. They were living life but always longing, yearning, and searching.

As Everett quietly walked down the dark hallway, he thought about his other useful warriors. He liked to refer to the members of humankind who helped him as warriors. They truly were warriors but lived out their lives without realizing the impact they might have on others. Small things they did mattered—making small talk with a new person at work, offering to help a struggling young family with a grocery bill, giving up a seat on the bus. Humans couldn't see the differences they made. Some made huge differences to people they had never met and wouldn't meet in their lifetime. Everett then directed his attention to Kelsey.

Kelsey was thirteen when his drunken father came home late one evening and began slapping him for forgetting to leave the porch light on. From there, his father brutally beat him with a broken shovel handle. In his drunken fit, his father clubbed him one last time, knocking him over an end table, where Kelsey lay passed out from the thrashing. Kelsey's mother screamed, begged, and pleaded for the beating to stop, which it did for Kelsey, but his father turned on Kelsey's mother with a vengeance. He raped, beat, and kicked Kelsey's mother without mercy and then threw her down a stairwell. Unable to get up or call for help, she slowly died of her injuries.

Four hours later, when Kelsey woke from being knocked unconscious, he found his dead mother at the bottom of the stairwell. His father was sitting in a blood-covered chair with half his head blown against the wall from a self-inflicted shotgun blast.

From there, Kelsey found himself in and out of children's homes, occasional foster homes, and maybe a relative's home for a weekend. That was Kelsey's life until he was seventeen and ran away. To get out, he faked his age to join the army and signed up for an assignment that got him as far away as possible, which happened to be the front line of the Vietnam War.

He saw horrors beyond description. His last mission found him hiking with his platoon through a rice field, when he stepped on a land mine that took his right lower leg and two of his fingers. If ever there were someone who could have justified climbing into a bottle and never coming out, it was Kelsey.

But he didn't. Kelsey's father had taught him one lesson: Kelsey vowed never to even taste a drop of alcohol. Even through the horrors of the Vietnam War, even with his brothers-in-arms taunting him and encouraging him to drink with them, he never did. He never drank, never tried any type of drugs, and never smoked. Hidden in the deepest corners of his character was a determination that he would be different. He wanted to do whatever it took to live a life as far from his father's life as possible.

During his months of physical rehabilitation at a VA hospital, Kelsey became friends with a chaplain who came to visit. First, the chaplain would read magazine articles to Kelsey, and as they become more comfortable together, sometimes they would play cards or a board game. At some point, the kindhearted chaplain spoke to Kelsey about heaven and his thoughts about the afterlife. That segued into talking about Jesus and the Christian beliefs of salvation. Kelsey was all in. He could not get enough of the wonderful message and the hope it promised. After the war, he stayed in Vietnam to help rescue the young nurse who had helped him through therapy. Newly married, together they traveled back to the place Kelsey had vowed he would never return to.

One house down from where he'd watched both of his parents die, he and his wife raised three girls. Because of his time spent in the military, Kelsey thought about a career as a police officer. He applied to the academy, where he continually struggled with the physical demands of the training. Despite encouragement from his fellow cadets, he had to face the cold reality that he couldn't meet the physical requirements. After struggling a bit to find employment, Kelsey was able to land a job working for the city as a custodian. Some in his position might have been bitter about the hand dealt to them, but Kelsey was always grateful. His three daughters all became schoolteachers. His wife was still a nurse. He enjoyed working, even though his leg pained him every waking hour. He thanked God every single day for the soft-spoken chaplain who'd quietly talked to a mentally and physically injured soldier in the jungles of Vietnam. Kelsey was always on the lookout for people who were damaged and in need of love, as he'd been years ago.

Everett smiled to himself as he looked out the window of the train station. The weather had changed again to a snowstorm. Everett knew it would take a lot of trust to see the big picture: two scruffy characters in the middle of a snowstorm, with no coats, one bloody, staggering into a train terminal in the middle of the night.

But Everett knew Kelsey.

Everett was with Kelsey as he lay on the kitchen floor after his father beat him. He was with him in the stifling, humid jungles of Vietnam. He was there holding his hand as Kelsey's leg was sawed off. He would be there again watching as Kelsey. Everett was confident Kelsey would come through again. Everett indeed knew Kelsey.

Kelsey loved his life. He loved his work. He was in love with God, the God who'd loved a broken, damaged youth and sent his Son as a sacrifice to a damaged world. Kelsey loved thinking about that as he worked. He reached for some compound and then proceeded to tackle a stubborn scuff on the tile floor.

To an outsider, Kelsey's job might have seemed unskilled, mind-numbing, and humdrum, but Kelsey was grateful. He had never been laid off. Even though he would never be anywhere close to rich and probably would work until the day he died, Kelsey was eternally thankful for the opportunity to clean the office buildings for the city. He normally cleaned the east and south police stations, but for the last two weeks, he'd been subbing in the train station. He was thankful it was his last night because he missed the guys at the police stations. Kelsey usually worked second shift, working every other day at each station. The officers were what made the job—good stories and good men and women. He decided he might knock off a little early there and stop by for a quick visit.

Everett knew he would leave Charlie, knowing what a strange sight he had prepared for Kelsey. He knew Kelsey was about done with his shift. He knew Kelsey would look up to see a lone man in the station—a man wearing a yellow T-shirt during a snowstorm.

Indeed, as Everett knew, Kelsey looked up from compounding the scuff to see a man standing in the abandoned train station. Kelsey murmured to himself, "Looks like he's been fighting." Then he thought, *Maybe he's been robbed. No, no. Why would he be wandering around in a blizzard with no coat? No one robs you of your coat. Fighting in the bar a couple blocks away.* Kelsey shuddered, as he had seen that scenario play out many times. *Ragged yellow T-shirt and bandages on his knuckles. Pants ripped. Looks like this fellow took a pretty good clock to the head Yeah, no doubt about it. This guy has been fighting, and from the looks of it, he's not much of a fighter.*

Kelsey wouldn't be knocking off early to go exchange any stories with the guys now that, minutes before the station was to close for the evening, a man without a coat had shown up.

Everett nodded with approval as he heard Kelsey quickly pray, *Well, God, what do you want me to do?*

Kelsey then thought to himself, *Poor fella. Probably just trying to get out of the storm.* Kelsey was new to such a dilemma. *How can I send this guy back out into that mess without a coat?* He knew he couldn't.

Kelsey knew what he should do. He went to the janitor's closet, reached for his own winter coat, and then headed back to the person he believed was a poor man who needed a coat.

CHAPTER 11

EVERETT THINKING AND BRIAN, THE CRUISER, AND THE SHOTGUN

Everett knew that evil never rested. It seeped into the fabric of human life slowly. It was like a constantly blowing wind. It waited for opportunities to slowly destroy and discourage. Evil wanted to extinguish its bitter enemies, which were hope, faith, and love. The swirling darkness of pure and relentless hatred was seemingly everywhere. It stalked humanity without mercy, lurking in the darkness, waiting to seize an opportunity to gain even the smallest of footing with an individual.

Once it had established a grip, evil would dig. It would burrow into that person like a constant tick or lice, infesting the life of the carrier, slowly spreading its rotting cancer into the soul. If a person became infected with the terrible disease, of course he or she would take notice, or loved ones would notice. But evil's biggest asset was its ability to destroy without the person realizing his or her soul was decaying. Evil had no greater goal than to take human souls from the almighty God of heaven. Evil especially enjoyed taking those who had known God.

Evil had gotten a foothold on Brian Michaels. He was rotting from the inside.

Everett had faced evil of all sizes. He sensed a movement; evil was stirring. He hoped his prayer warrior would not weaken. He thought to himself, *I know you are weary, but I need your prayers tonight. Soon you will come home.*

The evil one who had come to the café to hunt Brian would not be easily deterred. He would try again. He was assigned to capture. He was appointed to destroy. He'd spent much time on this target. He would wait in the shadows and then pounce and strike a depressing blow, cutting the mortal down with one swift blow. He would steal the man away that night into his master's lot. He waited in the shadow like a mutinous fog, ready to smother and suffocate.

Everett could sense Brian's despair.

At that moment, Brian was leaving the café. He walked the short distance to his squad car and thought about his pitiful life. What had become of his dream? Where had his life gone? He was never going to make captain. He knew it. Everyone around him knew it too.

Brian knew his wife didn't respect him. She blamed him for the death of their son. He'd been the cause. He hadn't done enough. He could have used some of his contacts to get their son more help, but he hadn't. He was lazy. He'd just gone to the hospital every day to watch his son die. *I have arrested criminals who are better men than you*, Brian thought.

As he sat down in the driver's seat, he noticed the government-issued shotgun holstered between the seats. He studied the weapon. He slowly opened the glove box. There sat an unopened box of shells. He unfastened the box and withdrew a single shell. He held up the shell to examine it in the dim light and felt it, carefully running his thumb over the casing, feeling the crowd-control pellets under the plastic. He smelled the shell.

It was cold in the car. Brian could see that his breath had fogged up and then frozen on the windshield and driver's door.

He stared at the gun again. He knew what he had to do. He was a loser. He hadn't done a thing in his life to benefit a single person.

Brian unlatched the gun's holster, eased the steel from the leather hatch, and laid the gun carefully on the passenger seat.

He again eyed the shell and then carefully placed it into the chamber of the gun.

CHAPTER 12

CHARLIE MEETS KELSEY

The train station was a welcome relief from the nasty snowstorm.

Everett told Charlie, "Sit tight," before heading down a dark corridor. The train station seemed deserted except for a lone custodian emptying the trash containers and sweeping under a ficus tree.

Charlie knew he should trust Everett's plan, but he still walked over to the arrivals-and-departures board to see what the train schedules were. As he'd somewhat expected, there were no trains due in or out of the station till tomorrow morning.

Charlie checked again—not a single train due in the station.

Meanwhile, Everett was nowhere to be seen. Over the loudspeaker, an announcement blared out: "Customers, the station will be closing in fifteen minutes."

Charlie looked around for Everett. He was again ashamed of himself for panicking. While he'd seen things no one of that world had seen, he felt himself starting to worry about what to do next.

Charlie had caught the eye of the custodian. Sitting near the window as the snow outside came down at an alarming rate, Charlie closed his eyes. *Why do humans worry? Why fret over trivial matters? Does God take care of the little sparrow?*

Does he not have a plan for each of us? Does he not want good things for us?

Charlie knew these answers. He smiled and thought of his home—his real home.

He thought of heaven and his first encounter and recalled with fondness his first time meeting Jesus.

As he sat on the bench in the deserted train station, Charlie didn't want to open his eyes. He wanted to die again and again to experience that love.

As soon as Charlie found himself on the beach, he knew he was in heaven, and looking over the vast ocean, he knew it was but a tiny portion of the immense paradise. It certainly wasn't all of heaven.

He immediately saw some similarities to his previous world, such as the ocean's waves tumbling onto the brilliant white sand. He heard seagulls soaring overhead. Warm sand squeaked as Charlie padded along the shoreline. The soft, powdery sand felt floury, soothing to touch, and was magnificent to gaze upon. A mountain range with lush foliage crowded its way onto the beach. Everything seemed fresh and new. There was an aliveness to everything. The colors and warm ocean breeze refreshed his senses with each wispy touch.

The comforting, repetitive crash of the waves sounded new—intense compared to the familiar. The beach was the same but different and different but the same—totally new and totally different but familiar. Had Charlie been there before? Was that home? He'd been away, but was he home now? He felt as if he were coming back to his childhood home and seeing the familiar through new eyes. But the former was the unfamiliar, and now Charlie had to reacquaint himself. He had been an alien in a foreign land, and now he had come home.

His old world had seemed so important until he'd witnessed the real one.

Up the shoreline, casually walking toward him, was a man. Charlie recognized him. Even from that distance, he knew the man. It was Jesus.

Charlie ran to meet him, though when the time came for them to be face-to-face, he couldn't look upon him. Charlie did not deserve to be in his presence and meekly fell down at his feet. He couldn't even open his eyes. He could only whisper two tiny words: "I'm sorry."

Jesus, in his eternal compassion, touched Charlie's shoulder and gently spoke. "Well done, faithful servant. Get up. Walk with me."

As Charlie rose, he opened his eyes and saw that Jesus was barefoot. His feet were scarred. Jesus took Charlie's hand, revealing marks on his wrists as well.

Jesus spoke again. "I'm glad you are here. Walk with me along the beach, and I will answer some of your questions."

It was then that Charlie really looked at Jesus. He had expected him to be wearing a flowing white robe, but instead, Jesus wore red gym shorts and a sleeveless black workout shirt. Jesus smiled, sensing Charlie's astonishment. He kindly spoke. "I thought after some questions are answered, we might take a jog up the coastline. I know how you used to love running."

Charlie stood dumbfounded, not saying a word. He felt a sheepish smile draw across his face. He was delighted to walk with Jesus.

They strolled quietly along the shoreline, and Charlie was awestruck by his presence. There he was, walking with a friend— his friend. After all the sermons Charlie had heard and all the Sunday school lessons, he was on a lush beach, nonchalantly walking with Jesus.

He remembered thinking, in his former life, that if he ever got a chance to walk with Jesus, he would have a thousand questions. But he didn't. He was content just to walk. The ocean's pacifying melody tumbled near their feet. The wind's gentle breeze whispered a carefree sonnet throughout the landscape. The mountains' bold dark green foliage curtained new discoveries, beckoning fresh experiences. He was walking with his friend.

Charlie was complete.

Jesus broke the peaceful silence, saying, "What flavor are you going to try?"

Charlie noticed they had veered slightly off the beach onto a grassy area where a small ice cream wagon stood. A man in a traditional white ice cream vendor uniform happily stood behind the wagon, ready to serve. Jesus spoke to him in a foreign language, and the man excitedly pointed to one of the tubs of ice cream and enthusiastically spoke to Jesus in the same mysterious language.

Jesus turned to Charlie. "Marcus tells me he has created a nice pistachio with flakes of chocolate. Sounds interesting."

Charlie just stood there. Jesus smiled, turned to the ice cream vender, and spoke to him again in the same strange language. The vender snapped to work and produced two ice cream cones. Jesus took them and handed one to Charlie.

Out of all the questions Charlie had thought of and all the answers he sought, oddly, the first question he asked Jesus was, "There's ice cream in heaven?"

Jesus laughed. "Of course. How could it be heaven without gelato?"

It's not that you can't remember your former life, Charlie thought, *but the former life seems so small. Even for the person who lives to be a hundred years old, life is such a fleeting mist. A momentary vapor. Here and then gone.* Did that mean life was trivial? Not important? Not at all. But once Charlie entered heaven, he could see that the things humans pursued in the world were so small. A red convertible Corvette that seemed to be such a lofty possession or a vacation home in the mountains, overlooking the lake, for example, which they toiled to obtain, was so small.

Charlie understood now. The grandest of possessions in the world were worthless there. *The love shown and the people you touch are what is important. Is there any greater power than love? No, there is not. The overwhelming love God has cannot be described. The love of God is absolutely boundless. It is forever. It has no end. Love God; love others. All the rest is piddling.*

He walked along the beach, eating a gelato cone, mesmerized. When Jesus talked, it was pleasant and comforting. It was cheerful, with a touch of humor, but still calming. It seemed natural for Charlie to put his arm around him, and then Charlie placed his head on his shoulder as they walked.

Jesus patted softly and then said again, "I'm glad you're here."

They had walked some distance, and the soft sand had gradually turned to coral.

Jesus said, "I know you have many questions, so ask me one."

Charlie no longer yearned for answers about his past life. He now had questions about his new world. He stopped, looked directly into Jesus's compassionate eyes, and said, "Since I have arrived here, I keep thinking I hear a woman singing."

Jesus smiled and then laughed. He instructed Charlie to sit down on a large rock, and together they sat, watching the ocean's tireless motion, with the surf crashing in and then drawing out. The next surf clangored in to the shore, and the ocean retrieved it back. It was soothing to see and more soothing to hear. Charlie then received his first lesson from the greatest teacher.

Jesus began by asking, "Do you know why the sound of the ocean is soothing? Do you know why it's so comforting to sit and watch the ocean? Why is mankind drawn to the ocean? Why do you believe man finds comfort in these things? Who placed in him this curiosity? Who, while the world was forming, placed in all men and women the yearning to know their Creator?"

Jesus spoke barely above the sound of the ocean waves, barely a loud whisper. Charlie leaned in closer to absorb his every word.

Jesus continued. "Who made the man who watches the waters? Who made the mighty ocean that crashes onto the earth? Mankind knows there is a beautiful rhythm to the ocean. Mankind has in his system a yearning for this lovely melody. Mankind is designed with an empty spot in his being. This empty spot can only be filled by knowing the almighty God of the universe."

Jesus stopped and turned his focus behind them, and Charlie instinctually followed his glance. From the tall grass strolled a cat.

Jesus sang out a melody, presumably to the cat, which broke into a run and bounded onto Jesus's lap. He patted the black-and-white cat, scratched behind her ears, and then handed the cat to Charlie.

"Roxie!" Charlie exclaimed. He immediately recognized his long-lost best friend. The cat from Charlie's childhood curled into a ball on his lap, expecting to be pampered and spoiled, just as in days long gone by. Charlie brushed her silky short-haired coat. Her loud purring announced her contentment, just as it had as they sat in Charlie's treehouse or on the porch swing.

Jesus smiled and continued. "Mankind forever longs to fill this void. Mankind is looking. Humans are drawn to the ocean. To the mountains. To the wonders of the God-made world. Even, for some, their pets."

Jesus reached over and gently stroked Roxie's belly. She in turn relaxed onto her back. "Don't you remember reading that in heaven, there are continuous praises being brought up? What you are trying to hear is the ocean praising God on every wave. What you are hearing that you interpret as a woman's voice is the ocean's song of worship. Other times, with deep bass sounds, to the beginner, it might be taken as a man's voice. Other times, it is the ocean's wonderful instruments of praise. You and mankind have lost the ability to listen, but it has always been there. Everything here—the ocean, the trees, all these things—praises God continuously. They also do in your former world, except at this time, that world is cursed."

Jesus moved his scratch to beneath Roxie's chin. "You are now learning again how to listen. Sit quietly, close your eyes, and listen to the mighty ocean praising God. So we did. I began to hear praises and shouts of joy from this mighty ocean. Just one of infinite shorelines where the surf crashes in and then retreats to start a new song forever and ever. Always new and always fresh."

The words became a wind that swept through Charlie.

Jesus continued. "Remember how pleasing it was to hear the ocean's waves? How soothing the sound? People are drawn to the ocean because they want to be near God. Why does a campfire relax you? Why do you consider the dark, glowing embers with reflection of delight? The deep-orange-and-blue campfire itself is praising God. Why does mankind stare with wonder upon the sunset? Why are humans drawn to the sunrise? Why, for countless generations, has mankind gazed at the stars with awe and amazement?

"It is because mankind is designed to praise his eternal maker, God. Yet mankind, for the short term, has chosen to separate himself from the Creator. These, though, did not forget. The truly mighty of your world. The sun, the water, the wind, the earth—they have not forgotten; they continuously worship. The mighty ocean has not forgotten. Listen again to its song. Hear again the majestic worship, the ocean shouts. Hear the song of the ocean echo throughout the landscape."

Again, they sat quietly. Charlie's ears were renewed by the beautiful music echoing deep into the mountain range.

Jesus continued. "The waves are crashing cymbals. A thundering chorus of jubilation springs from the mighty whitecaps. A soft flute melody pours from the receding foaming surf. All humans have a desire to know their God. They all have an emptiness they long to fill. Some fill the void with petty and shallow desires of the damaged world. The wise seek the God of the universe, the Maker of all heaven and earth. Everything here is in constant worship. That is the constant song, the continuous display of joy and exhortation from everything here. This is heaven. This is your home."

Jesus stood and pointed up the shoreline. "There is much you must learn. You have been assigned a guide to help you. And here he comes now."

Charlie lifted his gaze to see an old man meandering toward them.

Jesus said, "This is Everett. He is a trusted and loyal angel. He is very powerful."

Charlie had to look again to see if he might have looked the wrong direction.

He hadn't.

Awkwardly rambling along the shoreline was an older man in a ruffled cardigan sweater who looked out of place. His khaki pants looked as if they had been dragged by a truck. Charlie watched as Everett stopped, knelt to lift a flat rock, and then clumsily tried to skip it across the ocean. The rock plopped into the water without a single hop.

As Everett turned back toward Jesus and Charlie, a gust of wind lifted his thinning hair, whipping it from side to side, before the whole mess rested down over his eyes. Charlie watched, flabbergasted, as Everett slowly palmed the strings of hair back to one side. At that point, Charlie realized that death couldn't kill his sharp sense of sarcasm. Before Charlie could rein in his loose tongue, he blurted out, "Are you sure about this one?"

Jesus smiled as he spoke. "Lesson two: you can never judge by appearances." He added as he patted Charlie's back, "Yes. I am very sure about this one."

The loud bellow of a clock bell bolted Charlie back to the station, and he opened his eyes to see Everett standing in front of him. He was smiling. Charlie smiled back.

Everett spoke softly. "We are here for two missions, and one is to show you the hidden hand of almighty God. There are many times in a person's life when God is working, but most of the time, people ignore God's diligent work. God places people into lives to show his love. Even you are blind to this. You are seeing God in action, but you will ignore it. Even you."

Everett opened a duffel bag and drew out a large winter coat. He handed it to Charlie and then reached into the bag and brought out a new pair of heavily insulated boots, which he also handed to Charlie.

As Everett handed him the coat, Charlie smiled and noticed that it had a hood. The boots were well insulated and certainly better equipped than his tennis shoes to battle the ensuing blizzard the two would soon face.

Is this God in action? Charlie thought as the custodian, with coat in hand, approached the two.

The custodian was pleasant when he said, "Folks, the station is getting ready to close for the evening. I must ask you to leave." He paused and then timidly asked, "Do you have someplace to get out of this weather?"

Everett immediately spoke up. "Oh, sure. We just stopped to get a few things outta the locker. Boy, that storm caught us off guard. We had planned to take in a Rangers game, but different plans have come up."

Charlie hadn't known angels were such sports fans, but apparently, they were huge fans of all sports. Everett unzipped his pocket to reveal two flashy tickets. He studied them briefly and then handed them to the custodian. "Here. We're on our way out of town. Free tickets to Saturday's game."

"Oh, I can't take those." The stunned custodian took a step back.

"Well," Everett said, "they're going into the trash. We are on our way out of town. We must beat this weather. We are leaving now. There is a taxi at the door now to take us to the airport. If you don't take them, they will go to waste."

The custodian was dumbfounded. "Here. Let me pay you something for them. I just don't feel right taking them for nothing." He fumbled for his wallet.

"Nope. They're yours. Go to the game. Give them away. I don't care." He placed them in the shirt pocket of the speechless janitor.

The janitor shook Everett's hand profusely. "This is one of the nicest things anyone has ever done for me." He reached over to shake Charlie's hand as well.

Everett turned quickly and said to Charlie with a wink, "Let's get going. Taxi's here."

The custodian had a handful of crumpled bills and tried again to hand them to Everett, who would not accept them. Everett quickly headed to the door but turned to the custodian with one last bit of encouragement.

"Go Rangers!" Everett shouted.

With that, the two headed back out into the weather, which had become a full-fledged snowstorm. Just as predicted, a taxi was waiting, and now Charlie had a coat with a hood.

CHAPTER 13

CABBIE SCENE, INTERSECTION SCENE, SAM SCENE

As the car door slammed shut, Everett snapped back to the present situation and began conversing with the cab driver. "Do you know if the airport is still taking flights out?"

"Oh, I'm sure they are. It takes a lot to stop this city," the cabbie said in a slow Texas drawl. Then he relaxed into a slow, leisurely chat. "I'm having the hardest time getting used to this city life. Everyone seems to be in a terrible hurry. And you know what? They don't care what the weather or time of day is—hurry, hurry, hurry. I've been here about two months, and either I'm going to have to adjust, or I'm due for a nervous breakdown." The cabbie, tickled by his own clever line, burst into loud laughter. Still amused by his humor, he said, "Where you two headed out to on such a nasty night?"

Everett surprised Charlie when he said, "I'm heading down toward Houston."

The cabbie shrieked out loudly, "Yee-haw! That's where I'm from, neighbor. Well, not really Houston, but I'm a born-and-raised Texan."

As the signal light turned red, the cabbie felt the need to turn around to be sure they understood, and he leisurely and loudly said, "My little sister is a surgeon down in Houston. Smart as a firecracker. Always been smart. I'm telling ya, she makes the serious dough. I'm just proud as peaches for her. She's worked her tail off to get where she's at."

The light turned green as a snow plow blew through the intersection, spraying snow and slush all over the taxi's hood and windshield. The driver in the car behind them lay on the horn and then passed by, fishtailing through the intersection, still blaring the horn.

The cab crept slowly forward as the cab driver said, "See what I mean? Now, where is she going tonight? Why is she in an all-fire hurry to get there? See? I might just have that nervous breakdown. I need a vacation." The cabbie again howled with laughter. "I haven't even been on the job three months, and I need a vacation. How do you think my boss would like that?" he said, still chuckling.

Before anyone could respond, the cabbie answered his own question, speaking in his best eastern accent. "Are you crazy? A vacation? Get your sorry, sad sack back in that cab, and drive." It was a pretty poor impression but again seemed to amuse the cabbie, who slapped the dash, hopped up in his seat, and burst into another giggling fit.

Charlie looked to Everett, who seemed to be in a bit of a trance.

Everett was somewhere else. He had detected a severe hatred coming from the young woman who'd blared her horn as she passed by. She had an important role to play. Everett asked why she had such hatred and what she must do. His answer was revealed.

Samantha despised being called Sammy. She introduced herself to her business peers as Samantha and then granted them the pleasure of calling her Sam. If a person called her Sammy, she would dish out a slew of insults his or her way.

Sam cared about her career and not much else. She was determined to rise up the corporate ladder. Her grades at Michigan were outstanding. What kept her from being employed in the corporate world was her personality, which one interviewer described by saying, "I've met cacti who were friendlier."

For some reason, people couldn't handle her no-nonsense attitude. What did she care about Janet's new cat or Kevin's fourth grandchild? To be honest, she hadn't cared about the first grandchild. Pleasant people found new grandchildren heartwarming. Sam saw babies as irresponsible creatures who relied on everyone else to clean up their messes.

A month after graduation, a large corporation decided to take a chance on her. The boss was impressed with her transcript from Michigan and thought she could bring some young talent to the office.

One day the ladies of the office asked if Sam wanted to join them for lunch. When they said they were going to the local Mexican restaurant, she responded, "I don't run five miles a day to eat my weight in cheese dip. If you don't care about clogged arteries, be my guest."

In less than a week, most of the women of the office were plotting how to secretly poison her low-fat soy latte. The women who weren't in on the plot were on vacation.

The men either were terrified of her or schemed about how to loosen the window of her office so that when she leaned on the glass, she would fall the twenty-nine floors to the street below.

Sam had been raised by her mother, who preached to her that there was no God. She told her, "Humans evolved. There is no proof of God. Science points to facts that cannot be denied. Besides, do you really want to follow a God who allows childhood cancer and children born with heart issues? A God that allows abuse? Would a loving God stand by as parents watch their children die in front of them? What kind of God is that?"

Her household believed in facts and logic. How logical was it to believe there was a guy in the sky who played with the world's people as if they were his personal action figures?

At the next signal light, the cab caught up with Sam's Toyota Corolla.

As the cabbie rattled on about the Rangers' season, Everett glanced over to witness Sam barking orders into her cell phone. She was shaking her fist, and as soon as the light changed, she blared her horn out of habit.

Sam hated God, but more than anything, she hated Christians, with their condescending remarks and their Bible-verse garbage pinned up in their offices. She despised any religion. Any mention of any religion made her skin crawl. Most people, when the subject of religion came up, chose to be cordial. That seemed to be Sam's weak link: she just couldn't keep her opinion to herself. The University of Michigan had failed to educate her on the importance of tact—which was one of the reasons she'd been let go at her last job.

Most new employees understood that there was a certain protocol to speaking up in a meeting. A new employee simply hadn't earned the right to speak up until asked for his or her opinion, especially on the matter of someone else's religion or personal beliefs. Sam did not realize that.

On Sam's second day of work, during an early morning meeting, one of the longtime secretaries announced that her twin brother had lost his long-term battle with cancer, so she would be taking off two weeks to attend the funeral and start the process of closing his estate. Those in the room offered condolences, assistance, and heartfelt sadness for their friend.

The secretary bravely said, "I'm comforted in knowing that he is no longer in pain and now can be with our parents in heaven."

Anyone with any kind of heart would have let the conversation move on, but Sam couldn't let that one slide without correcting the woman's ridiculous story. Coldly, she spoke up. "I'm glad your brother isn't in pain, but I grew out of the idea that there's a heaven at about age five. He is not with anyone. He's deceased."

Most in the meeting looked to see who would say something so cruel and immediately thought, *Who is this person? When did we hire such a heartless creep?*

In the evenings, Sam made a hobby out of reading outline articles and then heading to the comments section to disprove any outlandish thought of a know-it-all Christian. She found great pleasure in upsetting any Christian she could find. She wanted to seed doubt and fear and make life generally unpleasant for any Christian she came in contact with. In short, she wanted Christians to be as miserable as she was.

Sam recently had started working at the juvenile detention center for the city, where her personality was a bit of an asset. She had a no-nonsense approach to the teens who entered the center. She didn't care if some punk said he had to "show his street cred to that guy." No, if someone acted like an idiot, he ended up in juvenile detention with her. Her rattlesnake-like personality was what some needed. There was no one better for the troubled youth to have on their side when the odds were stacked against them.

Everett smiled to himself. He was proud that he served a God who loved everyone, even the ones who despised him.

CHAPTER 14

CHARLIE AND EVERETT ARRIVE AT THE AIRPORT

The streets of New York were never quiet, but considering the weather, Charlie and Everett made the trip rather quickly.

Everett and the cab driver seemed to instantly connect, chirping together like two parakeets in a cage. When they pulled up to the terminal, the driver seemed genuinely sorry to end the conversation, which had touched on the subjects of family, high school football, and chili.

Charlie and Everett departed the cab, but instead of heading into the airport, Everett marched toward the parking lot. The large walls of the airport buffered the blowing wind for the most part, but Charlie saw that the shield would end soon, and they would be hit with an onslaught of wintry blast from the storm.

Right before they were to face the monstrous wind, Everett turned to Charlie and said,

"You have witnessed the mighty hand of God tonight."

Charlie responded timidly, "I'm sorry, Everett, but I just didn't seem to see anything."

Everett smiled kindly back at him. "That's how God works. God could change people's thoughts, actions, and deeds miraculously. He chooses, though, to work through others. He wants more than anything your relationship. He wants you to trust him. He wants you to rely on him. God has revealed to me how this will play out, for only God knows all. Would you like to know how two were lost but tonight have been found?"

Charlie nodded meekly.

Everett patted him on the shoulder. "I will tell you, but you have a job to do. It is about time for you to return home. You are here to escort someone home with you."

Charlie thought immediately of Karen and said, "Everett, Karen seems so beneficial to the work. Why take her now?"

Without speaking, Everett stuck out his elbow, and Charlie looped his arm through Everett's. Everett drew Charlie closer to him and readied them to turn the corner and face the howling wind. Charlie braced himself for the blast—and was shocked when he turned the corner.

CHAPTER 15

THE PRAYER CHANNEL

Charlie was blinded by a white light instead of the howling winds and blast of blizzard fury he'd expected to receive. As he walked through the living curtain, he could feel himself purged of the filth and sin that had clung to him while he visited his former home. In an instant, Charlie knew he had been purified again, and he felt the refreshing, overwhelming love of almighty God coursing through his being. He turned to glance at Everett, who appeared the same as before, still without a heavenly body. Charlie still hadn't seen him or any other angel in heavenly form.

Everett picked up on Charlie's thoughts and casually spoke. "I want to speak to you while in a human image. Soon what we have experienced will fade. You will be enamored with this world, and your former world will dissipate. You will have the memory, but it will seem small. We are still in your former world in a sense. We are in what you might remember being called a parallel universe. This is where prayers travel. Prayers of saints and sinners are here. Some are strong; some are weak."

Everett turned to face Charlie and gently, with the tips of his fingers, brushed Charlie's eyes. Charlie opened his eyes to see bolts of light around them, traveling toward a distant target. Thousands, if not millions, of prayers in all imaginable colors blazed and shone as they streaked by. Some blazed intensely white; others sparked an emerald green. Some sizzled and arced as they shrieked by. Some of the brilliant prayer arrows howled with intensity, while some casually drifted by.

Everett continued. "Some of these prayers are weak; their color is frail and faded, and they meander slowly. But all prayers reach almighty God. It's where we get our strength to accomplish work. Constantly, angels of all designs travel in and out of your former world." He watched Charlie.

Charlie was fascinated by the prayer arrows. He inched closer to some of the more slowly moving prayers. Upon close inspection, he determined the sizzling and popping sounds were human voices. With some of the slow-moving prayers, it was easy to hear the individual's requests. Charlie, captivated, listened to the prayers as they drifted by.

Please, God, can I have a dog for my birthday?

Please help me not to be late to work again.

God, can you please make my boss catch the flu?

Please, God, help me to be able to pay my electric bill.

Everett knew his time had come to strike. He knew Charlie was not quite prepared to see what he must do, so for just a moment, he left Charlie to his newfound attraction.

CHAPTER 16

EVERETT CONFRONTS
THE DEMONS

Everett stood boldly outside Brian's squad car. He felt the howling cold all around him—not from the wintry blast that raged on in the human world but from the icy hatred that radiated from the demons who lurked in the shadows around him. Everett drew his massive sword, making no effort to conceal his presence. He knew demons and devils of every size and power surrounded him. He felt their loathing for him. He also felt the intense and unimaginable power of almighty God coursing through him. He would not be timid. He would not cower at the despicable beasts. He had been instructed to hold his position. He would stand his ground as he waited till his human collaborator arrived.

He had seen throughout history that God worked through humans. He was not allowed to strike until the battle cry had been shouted. As the demons grew more confident, Everett could hear them jeering and hissing at him from the darkness. Some of the boldest demons came into the light to openly taunt Everett.

Throughout the millennia, Everett had seen countless battles. He could never become battle-hardened, as a human might. He never wearied of his appointed duty to his Creator. He had seen miraculous victories. He had viewed humans reject the countless means of help sent to rescue them from the horrors of the world. Even though he had been designed to better understand the workings of almighty God, it troubled him that humanity didn't welcome God's assistance in the cursed world. Why wouldn't humanity seek to know the Creator of the universe?

As the mighty Everett confidently stood with his sword drawn, standing his ground beside the squad car, protecting Brian from bigger and more powerful demons, two demons approached out of the darkness to oppose him. He recognized them at once. One was the handsome man who had entered the diner to further depress Brian, except Everett saw him for what he was: a slithering demon of despair. He would always appear to Everett to be what he really was: a hating, jealous lump of despair. The other was one of the largest demons Everett had encountered in some time. It was Drakius. He had grown immensely in hatred since their last meeting.

Drakius lumbered forward. Everett could see hatred and misery pour off his body like sweat on a hot, humid afternoon. He watched as Drakius leaned against the driver's side of the police car and wrapped his ghoulish flesh over the left side of the car, completely engulfing the side. Slowly, he seeped into the cracks of the windows and doors into the cab of the squad car.

Everett shouted, "Stop!" but Drakius only laughed.

He then spat back at Everett, "You have lost. You have been outsmarted again. You have failed. Your human counterpart has been discouraged."

Everett looked back to the front door of the diner and watched as Karen came out. He watched in agony as a platoon of demons swarmed her, casting words of discouragement upon her. They threw helplessness, apathy, fear, and embarrassment at her, but the one that forced Karen to turn and head away from the squad car to her own car was the demon of busyness. Everett could hear Karen's thoughts: *This storm is nasty. I'll sure be glad to get home. I know Brian could use a friend. I was going to invite him and his wife over for dinner Friday, but I really should get home. I'll do it soon. I'm sure he's too busy anyway. I'll ask them over later this spring.*

Drakius's laughter brought Everett back to the business of Brian.

"You see, Everett, we planted small demons around your so-called mighty Christian warrior." He hissed with amusement. "She is weak. She is not obedient. She is easily distracted. She has failed. This pitiful policeman's soul is mine tonight. I have won. You have lost. Be gone."

But Everett stood his ground. As Drakius reveled in his victory, he failed to see Karen take out of her pocket a small note written on the back of a receipt by a stranger she had never seen before that night and would never see again. The small note of encouragement contained a few words that spoke directly to Karen's heart—just a few kind words. That was sometimes all it took: a few words.

Everett knew Karen could not see the battle raging for Brian's soul that night. He smiled as Karen turned toward the squad car. She walked with determination and, with all the skill knit into her soul before she was born, tapped on the passenger window of the police car. That was the battle cry; the tide had turned.

With a triumphant cry, Everett raised his mighty sword and struck the shoulder of Drakius. The startled Drakius let out a howling growl. Pus and decay poured from the wound. Drakius swiftly staggered back from the car. Everett again raised the mighty sword to strike, but before he could, he saw out of the corner of his eye a demon charging in with a raised ax. Everett sidestepped the attacker, and the assailant whirled around, ready to strike Everett. He poised the ax high above his head and smirked, ready to crush Everett's exposed temple.

Everett calmly looked down at the abdomen of the demon, where his mighty sword had already impaled the body of the now helpless demon. Everett gazed into the eyes of the demon and realized it was the demon man who'd entered the diner earlier. The demon struggled to free himself from the sword, which was burning white hot, melting the flesh and spirit of the demon into the pavement, where it was absorbed. The demon pleaded and howled with anguish, knowing its eternal fate had been sealed. With one quick upward thrust, Everett sliced the demon in two, and the two halves lay quivering for a moment before dissolving into dust.

With that, the legion of demons scattered into the night, howling and cursing profanities at Everett and almighty God. After making quick work of the band of demons, Everett was now free to stand guard over the car. He watched as the last of the demons, the wounded Drakius, left. Drakius turned one last time to curse and spit at Everett. Everett knew he'd won the skirmish. He heard his orders. He was now ready to return to Charlie.

CHAPTER 17

THE UNVEILING

Everett returned to Charlie's side and spoke quietly to him. "Tonight prayers have been answered. The vast majority of people—nonbelievers as well as Christians—don't even realize God is constantly at work in their lives. The majority of people go through their day thinking God is not answering prayers. Some have even come to the sad conclusion that God is dead. But almighty God is working all the time. Would you like to see?"

Charlie nodded, surprised. Everett then drew his hand across an invisible pane as though he were wiping water off a window. As if watching a 3-D movie, Charlie witnessed a car trudging along the snow-packed street they had just come from.

"This is the driver of the car that was behind us as we rode in the cab tonight. The driver's name is Sam; she is a newly hired youth director at the police station where Brian works. She is young, ambitious, and creative and thinks God doesn't exist. Tonight God was working in her life. Even as she cursed God, his gentle hand was there. Tonight, because of a slow, good-natured cab driver from Texas, her life was spared. Because the cabbie was intrigued by the stories from the passenger in the backseat, he moved just a little slower. She could have zipped into the intersection tonight and been struck and killed by the speeding snow plow. Instead, she is on her way to implement a mentoring program she just got approved. All night she has been cursing and swearing at God for making her life more miserable than she deserves. All night God has directed us to protect her, to see her safely to her destination. She also is being used by God. He longs to use her more; she is a valuable asset. But the choice is hers alone. God never forces or demands. He always waits."

The picture of Sam faded, and Everett again swiped the fog to reveal another character of the evening. Charlie recognized the custodian they had met at the train station.

Kelsey was on the phone, and Charlie could see sadness on his face as Kelsey spoke into his phone.

"This is Kelsey, whom we encountered earlier. Kelsey is a faithful servant of almighty God. Even you did not recognize God's hidden hand at work. You misinterpreted Kelsey's actions this evening. You thought he was rushing out the door with coat in hand to try to beat the weather, when in fact, he was there to offer you his only winter coat. Kelsey was willing to give his coat to a total stranger."

They watched as Kelsey, on the phone with his wife, said joyfully, "Honey, you will not believe my luck. Right at closing time, a stranger gave me two tickets to the Rangers game on Saturday night."

"Kelsey's celebration tonight was short-lived, though," Everett said. "His wife reluctantly had to remind him that this Saturday night, he promised to take her out to a fine restaurant. Although he pleaded and begged to reschedule, she insisted. Kelsey finally accepted defeat and softly told his wife of thirty-plus years that he loved her and would be home shortly. He had planned to head to the police station to brag to the gang about his good fortune. Instead, he is now going to give his tickets away to the first officer he sees. What he doesn't know is that at this moment, his faithful wife is on the phone with their oldest daughter, sobbing. She feels she just broke the heart of the man she loves. She confesses she's not very good at this secret business."

Everett paused and then faced Charlie to continue. "Kelsey might feel low. He might feel sad. He also might feel he will never get a break in life. Like most of humankind, he doesn't realize that God is already at work. Kelsey will be getting a far bigger gift than a couple of hockey tickets. Kelsey, always in tune to the leading of almighty God, is going to the station to give away some tickets to one of his buddies. He will first see Brian reaching the door at the same time. He will unselfishly pass on his good fortune to another."

Charlie and Everett gazed into the lens and watched as the future unfolded. They saw that Kelsey's daughters and their husbands had flown in to surprise Kelsey at the restaurant. As they sat around a large table, Kelsey's oldest daughter stood up to make an announcement.

"Dad, we're sorry you missed the hockey game."

Kelsey shrugged nonchalantly and bellowed out, "I'll miss the whole season to have everyone sitting around the table with me!"

The crowd cheered and said, "Amen."

One of the sons-in-law laughed and said, "Yeah right."

Kelsey was elated to see his girls.

"Daddy, I have an announcement to make," the eldest daughter said. Then she exclaimed, "Daddy, you're going to be a grandpa!"

Shrieks, clapping, and hoots abounded as Kelsey frantically turned left and right, asking again and again, "What? What did she say?"

Most of the family laughed and united to say, "You're going to be a grandpa!"

"Her due date is on Kelsey's birthday," Everett told Charlie. "And in fact, she will give birth to the first grandchild of the family on Kelsey's birthday."

Kelsey was so overcome with joy that he sobbed uncontrollably. His oldest son-in-law playfully ribbed him, and then Kelsey, dazed with delight, hugged him and kissed him on the cheek. An onslaught of hugs and kisses from Kelsey then followed. He went around the table, hugging and kissing each member of his family, declaring to each how much he loved him or her.

Everett continued. "Many times, what humans might perceive as a low point in life is really a turning point. There was a great victory tonight I want to show you now."

Everett again swiped fog away and revealed a squad car in the parking lot of the diner they'd just visited. "The enemy meant great harm tonight, but because of powerful prayers, many souls have been saved. Many, many lives have been changed. Much good was done."

Charlie watched as a deathly soot crept over the left side of the squad car—a blackness so thick that no light could pass through. The creeping darkness lurked into the interior, over the seat, and around Officer Brian as he sat in the car.

"Watch the power of the Holy Spirit defeat the enemy," Everett said.

From the diner strolled Karen. There was a brilliant golden glow about her, a glorious radiance. As she approached the car, the darkness slithered back. She boldly went to the passenger window and tapped on the glass, making the darkness hastily retreat. The passenger door opened, and she climbed into the passenger seat.

The darkness vanished, replaced by the dazzling glow of gold.

"What really troubles Brian is loneliness," Everett said. "When his son died, he intentionally alienated himself from the world. He closed out the pleas of his wife, refused his friends, and spent years grieving the loss of his child. He let no one in. Until tonight. A simple invite to dinner. A reuniting of friends who used to play cards and go to the movies together. Tonight Brian's life is going to be turned upside down. He is turning one hundred eighty degrees, starting now."

As Karen got out and waved goodbye, a vivid glow lit the inside of the car.

"That is the spirit of the almighty God changing the heart of Brian," Everett said.

"What tonight was meant for wicked has been used for good. Brian was going to take his life but instead has decided to give his life. He has come back to the almighty God of the universe. He shortly will call his wife with excitement she has not heard from him for years. He will excitedly tell her Karen and Jay would like them to come over this Friday night for chili and cards. He will be so excited that he can hardly get the words out. All this is possible because Karen was equipped with the mighty spirit of almighty God. Karen answered the bidding of the Holy Spirit. A few simple words of encouragement scrawled on the back of a receipt by a stranger spurred her to action."

With that, Everett put his arm tightly around Charlie's shoulders and gently escorted him through a hazy fog.

They now stood in a nursing home. Nurses, aides, and doctors passed by without noticing the two spirits. Charlie felt the warm sun as it radiated through the large panes of glass onto his back. He surveyed the surroundings. Directly in front of them, an old woman in a wheelchair clutched a Bible resting on her lap. Her fingers, though feeble, traced the words of her tattered Bible. Wrapped in a blanket, she didn't look up, but Charlie saw her lips pantomiming the words on the page.

Everett spoke quietly. "No one here can see us or hear us."

A younger woman walked up to the older woman in the wheelchair. The young nurse's puffy, bloodshot eyes gave away a secret she had been trying all morning to conceal: she'd been crying. When the nurse saw that her favorite patient had declined throughout the night, the dedicated caregiver struggled frantically to compose herself. Large tears rolled off the nurse's cheeks and plopped upon the pages of the open Bible. The nurse tenderly kissed the forehead of the old woman, and again tears came, rolling off her face onto the old woman. The nurse lovingly dabbed them with a tissue and then again kissed the old woman.

The old woman let out a low moan. The loving nurse had brought a freshly warmed blanket to comfort the woman. As she removed the old blanket and carefully wrapped her in the fresh, warm one, the old woman moaned and then shrieked.

Everett spoke again. "The attending nurse is Casey's mother. She moved here to support herself and her son after her husband abandoned them four years ago. She is having what she thinks is the worst day of her life. She feels her world is crumbling around her, and by worldly standards, it is. Her only son was picked up last night by the police. She has just spent most of her night at the police station. The officer agreed to release Casey to her with the agreement that he will abide by the conditions set forth by the youth director, Sam. Again, sometimes what people might perceive as the lowest point is, in reality, the point where almighty God can turn something meant for bad into something great. This day will many times over be referred to as a great turning point in Casey's life. Casey will mention it many times—the day he met a policeman who was willing to take a troubled youth under his wing and talk to him about growing up. Years later, they both will share the story of the first time they met, when Casey was tased by the arresting police officer, who happened to be Brian."

Charlie then saw an image of Casey sitting in a jail cell.

Everett narrated. "Casey will be introduced to Sam. Because Casey is nineteen, in any other situation, he might have been sent to trial and sentenced. But because Sam is so tenacious and headstrong and wants to prove her worth to everyone, including herself, she will convince the powers that be that this one should be shown leniency, and he will catch a break. She will lobby hard to let this one prove he can right the ship."

Charlie watched the future story unfold before him. He saw Casey's mother leaving the jail crying. Casey tried to hold back tears, as he knew he had hurt his mother deeply. Entering the room next was Sam, who was far from sympathetic. She tore into Casey with the tenacity of a hungry wolverine, chastising him for his foolish decisions. She finally, with some despair, said she might be able to strike a deal if he had any chance of quickly securing a job.

At that moment, Casey's bloodshot eyes shone with a glimmer of hope. Earlier, as he'd sat pouting in the jail cell, bored, he'd gone through the pockets of the parka to find a business card from Martin's Bikesmith. On the back were the words "Always seeking talented technicians and sales reps." Casey sprang into action. He lied with such confidence and shrewdness that even the hard-core Sam was convinced. She snatched the card from his hand and scanned the back. The wheels turned quickly in her head as she thought about how she might be able to spring the kid out. "This might work," she said. "What's the possibility this bike shop will hire you?"

Charlie watched in amazement as Casey stood confidently and spoke with boldness as he again lied. "Oh, it's a done deal— more like orientation than an interview. Martin and I really hit it off." Casey glanced down at the ground, hoping that he had read the card right and that the shop was named Martin's Bikesmith and not Marty's or Mikey's or Mary's. Sam felt she had enough material to make a sound case and left to make her argument.

Everett stepped in to narrate more of the unfolding story. "Sam will argue her point about Casey and, more than anything, wear down the youth advisers, who finally will agree to lessen the charges if he can find gainful employment. Casey indeed will meet Martin the next morning and will be quickly hired.

Although their relationship will start off on rocky ground, over the years, it will develop into a close-knit friendship. Casey has the gift of conversation. Over the next several years, he will prove himself to be the best salesperson in the whole company, outselling even Martin in many years.

"During those years, Casey will meet a young postal worker whose route includes the bike shop. After a terrible first day on the job, she will think about throwing in the towel until a kind former postman says, 'Maybe I can help you.' Because of a stranger's kindness, she will decide to stick with her postal route, on which she regularly sees Casey at Martin's Bikesmith. After a few months of friendly banter, Casey will ask Eva to a date for ice cream. Their friendship will continue to grow, and eventually, Casey and Eva will get married.

"Martin will continue to influence young Casey's life, not only through business but also in friendship. When it comes time for Casey to go to college, Martin will step in and offer to pay all his expenses at Rutgers University. Though Casey will put up a fight, he will gladly accept, knowing it is his only chance to go to college.

"Martin will see it as an opportunity to repay the good fortune he received from his father to follow his passion of owning his own bike shop. Because of his father's gift to him to start his career, Martin will be happy to provide Casey with the same gift.

"Casey will grow up, go to college, and then become the adored pastor of an inner-city church. Many will be saved and comforted by the lessons he speaks to his community.

"Years into the future, Casey will visit Martin and his father after Martin's dear father has been given just a few days to live. Casey will offer to both a simple plan of salvation. Both men will accept this free gift. And after many years of emptiness, Martin finally will be fulfilled."

Everett paused and then continued. "As for Brian, his life was continued tonight. Today a friendship will spring forth between two wounded individuals. A lifelong friendship will be born for Brian and young Casey. Both have lost someone close. Both are lonely. Both are now at a place where the almighty God can work. Today Brian will see Casey for what he is: a shattered boy who needs someone to be there with him. Brian is now ready to become the man almighty God wants him to become.

"In a few evenings, they will go to a hockey game, using tickets given to Brian by a discouraged custodian. It will be Brian's first hockey game since losing his son. Even though going is difficult for him, he will bond even more with Casey at the game. Brian, the expert, will patiently explain to Casey the strategies, good plays, rules, and set plays. Casey will be interested in the sport, but he will be captivated by Brian.

"In a few days, Casey, longing for an excuse to see his friend again, will invite Brian to a small diner for coffee and free dessert, proud he can treat his new friend to a slice of pie. You see, Charlie, after Casey signs up for the mentoring program, the director will have mercy on him and let him keep the stolen coat. Casey will unzip a pocket to reveal two free-dessert coupons. Brian will be delighted to join him at his favorite diner. He will introduce Casey to a southern lady who works there. Karen, who has spent years counseling young men, will become yet another important person in Casey's young life."

Everett faced Charlie, his piercing green eyes seeming to look into the bottom of Charlie's soul. He smiled. "All this will happen because Casey's mother, four years ago, had a new patient come in the day she started. An old woman came in after suffering a stroke. She hasn't spoken in four years. Casey's mother noticed her read her Bible and pray. She asked the woman to pray for her son, who was perturbed at her for uprooting them and moving up north, where he knew no one. Each day, Casey's mother brought prayer requests to the old woman. Each day, the patient caregiver sat with her, brushing her hair, feeding her, or reading aloud a psalm. Even though the old woman never spoke, she heard her caregiver's request. She has taken the job of praying for Casey seriously. The old one has indeed listened.

"Even as her family pleads with almighty God to take her home, God has not, because she is doing what is asked of her. She has been praying without stopping for Casey. She has been praying for all the laborers of the harvest to become bold and for all those necessary to awaken again to the graces of almighty God. She has tirelessly searched her Bible for almighty God's promises. Some might think her moans and shrieks reflect her pain, but really, they come from the pain she feels in the lives of others. With much anguish, she tirelessly appeals to the almighty God for mercy in the lives and souls she lifts up. She is our great prayer warrior. Her mighty prayers have done much good for many."

Charlie looked at the old woman. Her tired, frail body shivered under the warm blankets tucked carefully over her.

Everett looked compassionately upon the old woman as he spoke. "I have guarded this one all her life. She has fought the good fight. Soon she will finish her race."

The kind caregiver brought a chair over to sit beside the old woman. Many years of servitude told the caregiver that the woman had little time left in the world. She tenderly held the woman's hand, caressing it softly, and the old one seemed to rally her strength. With great effort, she lifted her head.

Charlie could now see her face. Years of a constant positive outlook had etched deep smile lines into her face. Her worn face had a happy countenance upon it. She intently looked at something behind Charlie, and he turned to see what intrigued her: a bright red cardinal had lit upon a branch just outside. The caregiver watched the cardinal also, but the old one seemed to be focusing on something beyond.

Everett said, "She is looking for you. You see, Charlie, this is your mother. You have been brought here to escort your mother to heaven. Every day since you were taken from her, she has prayed to see you again."

"But my mother was young when I left," Charlie whispered.

"By this world's timeline, you have been away almost forty years. In heaven, there is no time. What might seem like years here on earth could only be considered moments in heaven."

Charlie gazed into the eyes of his dear mother. Her eyes seemed to lock onto his. She flashed a dazzling smile.

Charlie was about to say, "I think she sees me," when he heard a thunderous voice blast.

"Well done, good and faithful servant. Enter into his gates with thanksgiving."

Charlie turned in the direction of Everett, and there stood a mighty heavenly angel. The massive being stood well over twelve feet tall, and his legs and arms were like chiseled oaks. He wore solid-gold armor, and his cladding was of brilliant purple. Behind him, standing at attention, were a legion of angels. The massive being looked down upon Charlie, who recognized Everett's piercing green eyes.

Everett smiled, and his mighty legion of angels broke out into great cheers of jubilation.

From among the cheers and celebration of the mighty angels, Everett stepped forth in his majestic heavenly body to quietly announce to Charlie, "Your mother."

Charlie turned back to the old woman, but now standing before him, shining brilliantly white, was the mother of his childhood. He faced her and smiled.

"I've been waiting for you," Charlie said. He took her arm and turned to face the gates of heaven, where joy, rest, discoveries, and love would forever abound for those who accepted the free gift of salvation.

Printed in the United States
By Bookmasters